BY SHORE AND SEDGE

BY SHORE AND SEDGE

BY

BRET HARTE

Short Story Index Reprint Series

BOOKS FOR LIBRARIES PRESS
FREEPORT, NEW YORK

First Published 1885
Reprinted 1970

STANDARD BOOK NUMBER:
8369-3517-9

LIBRARY OF CONGRESS CATALOG CARD NUMBER:
72-121560

PRINTED IN THE UNITED STATES OF AMERICA

CONTENTS.

———◆———

AN APOSTLE OF THE TULES.

I.

On October 10, 1856, about four hundred
people were camped in Tasajara Valley,
California. It could not have been for the
prospect, since a more barren, dreary, monotonous, and uninviting landscape never
stretched before human eye; it could not
have been for convenience or contiguity,
as the nearest settlement was thirty miles
away; it could not have been for health or
salubrity, as the breath of the ague-haunted
tules in the outlying Stockton marshes swept
through the valley; it could not have been
for space or comfort, for, encamped on an
unlimited plain, men and women were huddled together as closely as in an urban tene-

ment-house, without the freedom or decency
of rural isolation ; it could not have been
for pleasant companionship, as dejection,
mental anxiety, tears, and lamentation were
the dominant expression; it was not a hurried flight from present or impending ca-
lamity, for the camp had been deliberately
planned, and for a week pioneer wagons had
been slowly arriving ; it was not an irrevo-
cable exodus, for some had already returned
to their homes that others might take their
places.   It was simply a religious revival of
one or two denominational sects, known as a
"camp-meeting."

A large central tent served for the assem-
bling of the principal congregation ; smaller
tents served for prayer-meetings and class-
rooms, known to the few unbelievers as
"side-shows;" while the actual dwellings
of the worshipers were rudely extemporized
shanties of boards and canvas, sometimes
mere *corrals* or inclosures open to the cloud-
less sky, or more often the unhitched cov-

ered wagon which had brought them there.
The singular resemblance to a circus, already
profanely suggested, was carried out by a
straggling fringe of boys and half-grown
men on the outskirts of the encampment,
acrimonious with disappointed curiosity, lazy
without the careless ease of vagrancy, and
vicious without the excitement of dissipation.
For the coarse poverty and brutal economy
of the larger arrangements, the dreary pan-
orama of unlovely and unwholesome domestic details always before the eyes, were
hardly exciting to the senses. The circus
might have been more dangerous, but scarcely more brutalizing. The actors themselves,
hard and aggressive through practical struggles, often warped and twisted with chronic
forms of smaller diseases, or malformed and
crippled through carelessness and neglect,
and restless and uneasy through some vague
mental distress and inquietude that they had
added to their burdens, were scarcely amusing performers. The rheumatic Parkinsons,

from Green Springs; the ophthalmic Fil-
gees, from Alder Creek; the ague-stricken
Harneys, from Martinez Bend; and the fee-
ble-limbed Steptons, from Sugar Mill, might,
in their combined families, have suggested a
hospital, rather than any other social assem-
blage. Even their companionship, which
had little of cheerful fellowship in it, would
have been grotesque but for the pathetic instinct of some mutual vague appeal from
the hardness of their lives and the helpless-
ness of their conditions that had brought
them together. Nor was this appeal to a
Higher Power any the less pathetic that it
bore no reference whatever to their respec-
tive needs or deficiencies, but was always
an invocation for a light which, when they
believed they had found it, to unregenerate
eyes scarcely seemed to illumine the rugged
path in which their feet were continually
stumbling. One might have smiled at the
idea of the vendetta - following Ferguses
praying for " justification by Faith," but

the actual spectacle of old Simon Fergus, whose shot-gun was still in his wagon, offering up that appeal with streaming eyes and agonized features was painful beyond a doubt. To seek and obtain an exaltation of feeling vaguely known as " It," or less vaguely veiling a sacred name, was the burden of the general appeal.

The large tent had been filled, and between the exhortations a certain gloomy enthusiasm had been kept up by singing, which had the effect of continuing in an easy, rhythmical, impersonal, and irresponsible way the sympathies of the meeting. This was interrupted by a young man who rose suddenly, with that spontaneity of impulse which characterized the speakers, but unlike his predecessors, he remained for a moment mute, trembling, and irresolute. The fatal hesitation seemed to check the unreasoning, monotonous flow of emotion, and to recall to some extent the reason and even the criticism of the worshipers. He stammered a prayer whose earnestness was undoubted, whose humility was but too apparent, but his words fell on faculties already benumbed by repetition and rhythm. A slight movement of curiosity in the rear benches, and a whisper that it was the maiden effort of a new preacher, helped to prolong the interruption. A heavy man of strong physical expression sprang to the rescue with a hysterical cry of " Glory!" and a tumultuous fluency of epithet and sacred adjuration. Still the meeting wavered. With one final paroxysmal cry, the powerful man threw his arms around his nearest neighbor and burst into silent tears. An anxious hush followed; the speaker still continued to sob on his neighbor's shoulder. Almost before the fact could be commented upon, it was noticed that the entire rank of worshipers on the bench beside him were crying also; the second and third rows were speedily dissolved in tears, until even the very youthful scoffers in the last benches suddenly found their

half-hysterical laughter turned to sobs. The
danger was averted, the reaction was complete; the singing commenced, and in a few
moments the hapless cause of the interruption and the man who had retrieved the dis-
aster stood together outside the tent. A
horse was picketed near them.

The victor was still panting from his late
exertions, and was more or less diluvial in
eye and nostril, but neither eye nor nostril
bore the slightest tremor of other expression.
His face was stolid and perfectly in keeping
with his physique, — heavy, animal, and un-
intelligent.

"Ye oughter trusted in the Lord," he
said to the young preacher.

"But I did," responded the young man,
earnestly.

"That's it. Justifyin' yourself by works
instead o' leanin' onto Him! Find Him,
sez you! Git Him, sez you! Works is
vain. Glory! glory!" he continued, with
fluent vacuity and wandering, dull, observant eyes.

"But if I had a little more practice in class, Brother Silas, more education?"

"The letter killeth," interrupted Brother Silas. Here his wandering eyes took dull cognizance of two female faces peering through the opening of the tent. "No, yer mishun, Brother Gideon, is to seek Him in the by-ways, in the wilderness, — where the foxes hev holes and the ravens hev their young, — but not in the Temples of the people. Wot sez Sister Parsons?"

One of the female faces detached itself from the tent flaps, which it nearly resembled in color, and brought forward an angular figure clothed in faded fustian that had taken the various shades and odors of household service.

"Brother Silas speaks well," said Sister Parsons, with stridulous fluency. "It's foreordained. Fore-ordinashun is better nor ordinashun, saith the Lord. He shall go forth, turnin' neither to the right hand nor the left hand, and seek Him among the lost tribes and the ungodly. He shall put aside the temptashun of Mammon and the flesh." Her eyes and those of Brother Silas here both sought the other female face, which was that of a young girl of seventeen.

"Wot sez little Sister Meely, — wot sez Meely Parsons?" continued Brother Silas, as if repeating an unctuous formula.

The young girl came hesitatingly forward, and with a nervous cry of "Oh, Gideon!" threw herself on the breast of the young man.

For a moment they remained locked in each other's arms. In the promiscuous and fraternal embracings which were a part of the devotional exercises of the hour, the act passed without significance. The young man gently raised her face. She was young and comely, albeit marked with a half-frightened, half-vacant sorrow. "Amen," said Brother Gideon, gravely.

He mounted his horse and turned to go. Brother Silas had clasped his powerful arms around both women, and was holding them in a ponderous embrace.

" Go forth, young man, into the wilderness."

The young man bowed his head, and urged his horse forward in the bleak and barren plain. In half an hour every vestige of the camp and its unwholesome surroundings was lost in the distance. It was as if the strong desiccating wind, which seemed to spring up at his horse's feet, had cleanly erased the flimsy structures from the face of the plain, swept away the lighter breath of praise and plaint, and dried up the easy-flowing tears. The air was harsh but pure; the grim economy of form and shade and color in the level plain was coarse but not vulgar; the sky above him was cold and distant but not repellent; the moisture that had been denied his eyes at the prayer-meeting overflowed them here; the words that had choked his utterance an hour ago now rose to his lips. He threw himself from his

horse, and kneeling in the withered grass —
a mere atom in the boundless plain — lifted
his pale face against the irresponsive blue
and prayed.

He prayed that the unselfish dream of
his bitter boyhood, his disappointed youth,
might come to pass. He prayed that he
might in higher hands become the humble
instrument of good to his fellow-man. He
prayed that the deficiencies of his scant education, his self-taught learning, his helpless
isolation, and his inexperience might be overlooked or reinforced by grace. He prayed
that the Infinite Compassion might enlighten
his ignorance and solitude with a manifes-
tation of the Spirit ; in his very weakness
he prayed for some special revelation, some
sign or token, some visitation or gracious
unbending from that coldly lifting sky. The
low sun burned the black edge of the distant
tules with dull eating fires as he prayed, lit
the dwarfed hills with a brief but ineffectual
radiance, and then died out. The lingering

trade winds fired a few volleys over its grave, and then lapsed into a chilly silence. The young man staggered to his feet; it was quite dark now, but the coming night had advanced a few starry vedettes so near the plain they looked like human watch-fires. For an instant he could not remember where he was. Then a light trembled far down at the entrance of the valley. Brother Gideon recognized it. It was in the lonely farmhouse of the widow of the last Circuit preacher.

II.

The abode of the late Reverend Marvin Hiler remained in the disorganized condition he had left it when removed from his sphere of earthly uselessness and continuous accident. The straggling fence that only half inclosed the house and barn had stopped at that point where the two deacons who had each volunteered to do a day's work on it had completed their allotted

time. The building of the barn had been
arrested when the half load of timber contributed by Sugar Mill brethren was exhausted, and three windows given by " Christian
Seekers " at Martinez painfully accented
the boarded spaces for the other three that
" Unknown Friends " in Tasajara had promised but not yet supplied. In the clearing
some trees that had been felled but not taken
away added to the general incompleteness.

Something of this unfinished character
clung to the Widow Hiler and asserted itself
in her three children, one of whom was con-
sistently posthumous. Prematurely old and
prematurely disappointed, she had all the
inexperience of girlhood with the cares of
maternity, and kept in her family circle the
freshness of an old maid's misogynistic an-
tipathies with a certain guilty and remorse-
ful consciousness of widowhood. She supported the meagre household to which her
husband had contributed only the extra
mouths to feed with reproachful astonish-

2

ment and weary incapacity. She had long since grown tired of trying to make both ends meet, of which she declared " the Lord had taken one." During her two years' widowhood she had waited on Providence, who by a pleasing local fiction had been made responsible for the disused and cast-off furniture and clothing which, accompanied with scriptural texts, found their way mysteriously into her few habitable rooms. The providential manna was not always fresh ; the ravens who fed her and her little ones with flour from the Sugar Mills did not always select the best quality. Small wonder that, sitting by her lonely hearthstone, — a borrowed stove that supplemented the unfinished fireplace, — surrounded by her mismatched furniture and clad in misfitting garments, she had contracted a habit of sniffling during her dreary watches. In her weaker moments she attributed it to grief ; in her stronger intervals she knew that it sprang from damp and draught.

In her apathy the sound of horses' hoofs at her unprotected door even at that hour neither surprised nor alarmed her. She lifted her head as the door opened and the pale face of Gideon Deane looked into the room. She moved aside the cradle she was rocking, and, taking a saucepan and tea-cup from a chair beside her, absently dusted it with her apron, and pointing to the vacant seat said, "Take a chair," as quietly as if he had stepped from the next room instead of the outer darkness.

"I'll put up my horse first," said Gideon gently.

"So do," responded the widow briefly.

Gideon led his horse across the inclosure, stumbling over the heaps of rubbish, dried chips, and weather-beaten shavings with which it was strewn, until he reached the unfinished barn, where he temporarily bestowed his beast. Then taking a rusty axe, by the faint light of the stars, he attacked one of the fallen trees with such energy that

at the end of ten minutes he reappeared at
the door with an armful of cut boughs and
chips, which he quietly deposited behind the
stove. Observing that he was still standing
as if looking for something, the widow lifted
her eyes and said, " Ef it 's the bucket, I
reckon ye 'll find it at the spring, where one
of them foolish Filgee boys left it. I 've
been that tuckered out sens sundown, I ain't
had the ambition to go and tote it back."
Without a word Gideon repaired to the
spring, filled the missing bucket, replaced
the hoop on the loosened staves of another
he found lying useless beside it, and again
returned to the house. The widow once
more pointed to the chair, and Gideon sat
down. " It 's quite a spell sens you wos
here," said the Widow Hiler, returning her
foot to the cradle-rocker; " not sens yer was
ordained. Be'n practicin', I reckon, at the
meetin'."

A slight color came into his cheek. " My
place is not there, Sister Hiler," he said

gently; "it's for those with the gift o'
tongues. I go forth only a common laborer
in the vineyard." He stopped and hesitated; he might have said more, but the
widow, who was familiar with that kind of
humility as the ordinary perfunctory expression of her class, suggested no sympathetic interest in his mission.

"Thar's a deal o' talk over there," she
said dryly, "and thar's folks ez thinks thar's
a deal o' money spent in picnicking the
Gospel that might be given to them ez wish
to spread it, or to their widows and children.
But that don't consarn you, Brother Gideon.
Sister Parsons hez money enough to settle
her darter Meely comfortably on her own
land; and I've heard tell that you and Meely
was only waitin' till you was ordained to be
jined together. You'll hev an easier time of
it, Brother Gideon, than poor Marvin Hiler
had," she continued, suppressing her tears
with a certain astringency that took the
place of her lost pride; "but the Lord wills
that some should be tried and some not."

"But I am not going to marry Meely Parsons," said Gideon quietly.

The widow took her foot from the rocker. "Not marry Meely!" she repeated vaguely. But relapsing into her despondent mood she continued: "Then I reckon it's true what other folks sez of Brother Silas Braggley makin' up to her and his powerful exhortin' influence over her ma. Folks sez ez Sister Parsons hez just resigned her soul inter his keepin'."

"Brother Silas hez a heavenly gift," said the young man, with gentle enthusiasm; "and perhaps it may be so. If it is, it is the Lord's will. But I do not marry Meely because my life and my ways henceforth must lie far beyond her sphere of strength. I ought n't to drag a young inexperienced soul with me to battle and struggle in the thorny paths that I must tread."

"I reckon you know your own mind," said Sister Hiler grimly. "But thar's folks ez might allow that Meely Parsons ain't any better than others, that she should n't have her share o' trials and keers and crosses. Riches and bringin' up don't exempt folks from the shadder. *I* married Marvin Hiler outer a house ez good ez Sister Parsons', and at a time when old Cyrus Parsons had n't a roof to his head but the cover of the emigrant wagon he kem across the plains in. I might say ez Marvin knowed pretty well wot it was to have a helpmeet in his ministration, if it was n't vanity of sperit to say it now. But the flesh is weak, Brother Gideon." Her influenza here resolved itself into unmistakable tears, which she wiped away with the first article that was accessible in the work-bag before her. As it chanced to be a black silk neckerchief of the deceased Hiler, the result was funereal, suggestive, but practically ineffective.

" You were a good wife to Brother Hiler," said the young man gently. " Everybody knows that."

" It 's suthin' to think of since he 's gone,"

continued the widow, bringing her work nearer to her eyes to adjust it to their tear-dimmed focus. " It 's suthin' to lay to heart in the lonely days and nights when thar 's no man round to fetch water and wood and lend a hand to doin' chores; it 's suthin' to remember, with his three children to feed, and little Selby, the eldest, that vain and useless that he can't even tote the baby round while I do the work of a hired man."

" It 's a hard trial, Sister Hiler," said Gideon, " but the Lord has His appointed time."

Familiar as consolation by vague quotation was to Sister Hiler, there was an occult sympathy in the tone in which this was offered that lifted her for an instant out of her narrower self. She raised her eyes to his. The personal abstraction of the devotee had no place in the deep dark eyes that were lifted from the cradle to hers with a sad, discriminating, and almost womanly sympathy. Surprised out of her selfish preoccupation, she was reminded of her apparent callousness to what might be his present disappointment. Perhaps it seemed strange to her, too, that those tender eyes should go a-begging.

"Yer takin' a Christian view of yer own disappointment, Brother Gideon," she said, with less astringency of manner; "but every heart knoweth its own sorrer. I 'll be gettin' supper now that the baby's sleepin' sound, and ye 'll sit by and eat."

"If you let me help you, Sister Hiler," said the young man with a cheerfulness that belied any overwhelming heart affection, and awakened in the widow a feminine curiosity as to his real feelings to Meely. But her further questioning was met with a frank, amiable, and simple brevity that was as puzzling as the most artful periphrase of tact. Accustomed as she was to the loquacity of grief and the confiding prolixity of disappointed lovers, she could not understand her guest's quiescent attitude. Her curiosity, however, soon gave way to the habitual contemplation of her own sorrows, and she could not forego the opportune presence of a sympathizing auditor to whom she could relieve her feelings. The preparations for the evening meal were therefore accompanied by a dreary monotone of lamentation. She bewailed her lost youth, her brief courtship, the struggles of her early married life, her premature widowhood, her penurious and helpless existence, the disruption of all her present ties, the hopelessness of the future. She rehearsed the unending plaint of those long evenings, set to the music of the restless wind around her bleak dwelling, with something of its stridulous reiteration. The young man listened, and replied with softly assenting eyes, but without pausing in the material aid that he was quietly giving her. He had removed the cradle of the sleeping child to the bedroom, quieted the sudden wakefulness of " Pinkey," rearranged the straggling furniture of the sitting-room with

much order and tidiness, repaired the hinges
of a rebellious shutter and the lock of an
unyielding door, and yet had apparently retained an unabated interest in her spoken
woes. Surprised once more into recognizing
this devotion, Sister Hiler abruptly arrested
her monologue.

"Well, if you ain't the handiest man I
ever seed about a house!"

"Am I?" said Gideon, with suddenly
sparkling eyes. "Do you really think so?"

"I do."

"Then you don't know how glad I am."
His frank face so unmistakably showed his
simple gratification that the widow, after
gazing at him for a moment, was suddenly
seized with a bewildering fancy. The first
effect of it was the abrupt withdrawal of
her eyes, then a sudden effusion of blood to
her forehead that finally extended to her
cheek-bones, and then an interval of forget-
fulness where she remained with a plate held
vaguely in her hand. When she succeeded

at last in putting it on the table instead of the young man's lap, she said in a voice quite unlike her own, —

" Sho ! "

"I mean it," said Gideon, cheerfully. After a pause, in which he unostentatiously rearranged the table which the widow was abstractedly disorganizing, he said gently, " After tea, when you're not so much flustered with work and worry, and more composed in spirit, we'll have a little talk, Sister Hiler. I'm in no hurry to-night, and if you don't mind I'll make myself comfortable in the barn with my blanket until sun-up to-morrow. I can get up early enough to do some odd chores round the lot before I go."

" You know best, Brother Gideon," said the widow, faintly, " and if you think it's the Lord's will, and no speshal trouble to you, so do. But sakes alive ! it's time I tidied myself a little," she continued, lifting one hand to her hair, while with the other

she endeavored to fasten a buttonless collar;
" leavin' alone the vanities o' dress, it 's ez
much as one can do to keep a clean rag on
with the children climbin' over ye. Sit by,
and I 'll be back in a minit." She retired
to the back room, and in a few moments returned with smoothed hair and a palm-leaf
broché shawl thrown over her shoulders,
which not only concealed the ravages made
by time and maternity on the gown beneath,
but to some extent gave her the suggestion
of being a casual visitor in her own household. It must be confessed that for the rest
of the evening Sister Hiler rather lent herself to this idea, possibly from the fact that
it temporarily obliterated the children, and
quite removed her from any responsibility in
the unpicturesque household. This effect
was only marred by the absence of any impression upon Gideon, who scarcely appeared
to notice the change, and whose soft eyes
seemed rather to identify the miserable woman under her forced disguise. He prefaced

the meal with a fervent grace, to which the
widow listened with something of the conscious attitude she had adopted at church
during her late husband's ministration, and
during the meal she ate with a like consciousness of " company manners."

Later that evening Selby Hiler woke up
in his little truckle bed, listening to the rising midnight wind, which in his childish
fancy he confounded with the sound of voices
that came through the open door of the living-room.   He recognized the deep voice of
the young minister, Gideon, and the occasional tearful responses of his mother, and
he was fancying himself again at church
when he heard a step, and the young preacher
seemed to enter the room, and going to the
bed leaned over it and kissed him on the
forehead, and then bent over his little brother
and sister and kissed them too.   Then he
slowly reëntered the living-room.   Lifting
himself softly on his elbow, Selby saw him
go up towards his mother, who was crying,

with her head on the table, and kiss her
also on the forehead. Then he said " Good-
night," and the front door closed, and Selby
heard his footsteps crossing the lot towards
the barn. His mother was still sitting with
her face buried in her hands when he fell
asleep.

She sat by the dying embers of the fire
until the house was still again; then she rose
and wiped her eyes. " Et 's a good thing,"
she said, going to the bedroom door, and
looking in upon her sleeping children; " et 's
a mercy and a blessing for them and — for
— me. But — but — he might — hev — said
— he —— loved me ! "

III.

Although Gideon Deane contrived to find
a nest for his blanket in the mouldy straw of
the unfinished barn loft, he could not sleep.
He restlessly watched the stars through the
cracks of the boarded roof, and listened to
the wind that made the half-open structure

as vocal as a sea-shell, until past midnight.
Once or twice he had fancied he heard the
tramp of horse-hoofs on the far-off trail, and
now it seemed to approach nearer, mingled
with the sound of voices. Gideon raised his
head and looked through the doorway of the
loft. He was not mistaken : two men had
halted in the road before the house, and
were examining it as if uncertain if it were
the dwelling they were seeking, and were
hesitating if they should rouse the inmates.
Thinking he might spare the widow this disturbance to her slumbers, and possibly some
alarm, he rose quickly, and descending to the
inclosure walked towards the house. As he
approached the men advanced to meet him,
and by accident or design ranged themselves
on either side. A glance showed him they
were strangers to the locality.

"We're lookin' fer the preacher that lives
here," said one, who seemed to be the elder.
"A man by the name o' Hiler, I reckon!"

"Brother Hiler has been dead two years,"

responded Gideon. "His widow and children live here."

The two men looked at each other. The younger one laughed; the elder mumbled something about its being "three years ago," and then turning suddenly on Gideon, said:

"P'r'aps *you're* a preacher?"

"I am."

"Can you come to a dying man?"

"I will."

The two men again looked at each other. "But," continued Gideon, softly, "you'll please keep quiet so as not to disturb the widow and her children, while I get my horse." He turned away; the younger man made a movement as if to stop him, but the elder quickly restrained his hand. "He isn't goin' to run away," he whispered. "Look," he added, as Gideon a moment later reappeared mounted and equipped.

"Do you think we'll be in time?" asked the young preacher as they rode quickly away in the direction of the tules.

3

The younger repressed a laugh; the other answered grimly, "I reckon."

"And is he conscious of his danger?"

"I reckon."

Gideon did not speak again. But as the onus of that silence seemed to rest upon the other two, the last speaker, after a few moments' silent and rapid riding, continued abruptly, "You don't seem curious?"

"Of what?" said Gideon, lifting his soft eyes to the speaker. "You tell me of a brother at the point of death, who seeks the Lord through an humble vessel like myself. *He* will tell me the rest."

A silence still more constrained on the part of the two strangers followed, which they endeavored to escape from by furious riding; so that in half an hour the party had reached a point where the tules began to sap the arid plain, while beyond them broadened the lagoons of the distant river. In the foreground, near a clump of dwarfed willows, a camp-fire was burning, around

which fifteen or twenty armed men were collected, their horses picketed in an outer circle guarded by two mounted sentries. A
blasted cotton-wood with a single black arm
extended over the tules stood ominously
against the dark sky.

The circle opened to receive them and
closed again. The elder man dismounted,
and leading Gideon to the blasted cotton-
wood, pointed to a pinioned man seated at
its foot with an armed guard over him. He
looked up at Gideon with an amused smile.

"You said it was a dying man," said Gideon, recoiling.

"He will be a dead man in half an hour,"
returned the stranger.

"And you?"

"We are the Vigilantes from Alamo.
This man," pointing to the prisoner, "is a
gambler who killed a man yesterday. We
hunted him here, tried him an hour ago, and
found him guilty. The last man we hung
here, three years ago, asked for a parson.

We brought him the man who used to live where we found you. So we thought we 'd give this man the same show, and brought you."

"And if I refuse ? " said Gideon.

The leader shrugged his shoulders.

"That 's *his* lookout, not ours. We 've given him the chance. Drive ahead, boys," he added, turning to the others; "the parson allows he won't take a hand."

" One moment," said Gideon, in desperation, " one moment, for the sake of that God you have brought me here to invoke in behalf of this wretched man. One moment, for the sake of Him in whose presence you must stand one day as he does now." With passionate earnestness he pointed out the vindictive impulse they were mistaking for Divine justice; with pathetic fervency he fell upon his knees and implored their mercy for the culprit. But in vain. As at the camp-meeting of the day before, he was chilled to find his words seemed to fall on unheeding and unsympathetic ears. He looked around on their abstracted faces; in their gloomy savage enthusiasm for expiatory sacrifice, he was horrified to find the same unreasoning exaltation that had checked his exhortations then. Only one face looked upon his, half mischievously, half compassionately. It was the prisoner's.

"Yer wastin' time on us," said the leader, dryly; "wastin' *his* time. Had n't you better talk to him?"

Gideon rose to his feet, pale and cold. "He may have something to confess. May I speak with him alone?" he said gently.

The leader motioned to the sentry to fall back. Gideon placed himself before the prisoner so that in the faint light of the camp-fire the man's figure was partly hidden by his own. "You meant well with your little bluff, pardner," said the prisoner, not unkindly, " but they 've got the cards to win."

"Kneel down with your back to me," said

Gideon, in a low voice. The prisoner fell on his knees. At the same time he felt Gideon's hand and the gliding of steel behind his back, and the severed cords hung loosely on his arms and legs.

"When I lift my voice to God, brother," said Gideon, softly, "drop on your face and crawl as far as you can in a straight line in my shadow, then break for the tules. I will stand between you and their first fire."

"Are you mad?" said the prisoner. "Do you think they won't fire lest they should hurt you? Man! they'll kill *you*, the first thing."

"So be it — if your chance is better."

Still on his knees, the man grasped Gideon's two hands in his own and devoured him with his eyes.

"You mean it?"

"I do."

"Then," said the prisoner, quietly, "I reckon I'll stop and hear what you've got to say about God until they're ready."

" You refuse to fly ? "

" I reckon I was never better fitted to die than now," said the prisoner, still grasping his hand. After a pause he added in a lower tone, " I can't pray — but — I think," he hesitated; " I think I could manage to ring in in a hymn."

" Will you try, brother ? "

" Yes."

With their hands tightly clasped together, Gideon lifted his gentle voice. The air was a common one, familiar in the local religious gatherings, and after the first verse one or two of the sullen lookers-on joined not unkindly in the refrain. But, as he went on, the air and words seemed to offer a vague expression to the dull lowering animal emotion of the savage concourse, and at the end of the second verse the refrain, augmented in volume and swelled by every voice in the camp, swept out over the hollow plain.

It was met in the distance by a far-off cry. With an oath taking the place of his suppli-

cation, the leader sprang to his feet. But
too late! The cry was repeated as a nearer
slogan of defiance — the plain shook — there
was the tempestuous onset of furious hoofs
— a dozen shots — the scattering of the embers of the camp-fire into a thousand vanishing sparks even as the lurid gathering of
savage humanity was dispersed and dissi-
pated over the plain, and Gideon and the
prisoner stood alone. But as the sheriff of
Contra Costa with his rescuing *posse* swept
by, the man they had come to save fell forward in Gideon's arms with a bullet in his
breast — the Parthian shot of the flying
Vigilante leader.

The eager crowd that surged around him
with outstretched helping hands would have
hustled Gideon aside. But the wounded
man roused himself, and throwing an arm
around the young preacher's neck, warned
them back with the other. "Stand back!"
he gasped. "He risked his life for mine!
Look at him, boys! Wanted ter stand up

'twixt them hounds and me and draw their fire on himself! Ain't he just hell?" he stopped; an apologetic smile crossed his lips. "I clean forgot, pardner; but it's all right. I said I was ready to go; and I am." His arm slipped from Gideon's neck; he slid to the ground; he had fainted.

A dark, military-looking man pushed his way through the crowd — the surgeon, one of the *posse*, accompanied by a younger man fastidiously dressed. The former bent over the unconscious prisoner, and tore open his shirt; the latter followed his movements with a flush of anxious inquiry in his handsome, careless face. After a moment's pause the surgeon, without looking up, answered the young man's mute questioning. "Better send the sheriff here at once, Jack."

"He is here," responded the official, joining the group.

The surgeon looked up at him. "I am afraid they've put the case out of your jurisdiction, Sheriff," he said grimly. "It's only a matter of a day or two at best — perhaps only a few hours. But he won't live to be taken back to jail."

" Will he live to go as far as Martinez?" asked the young man addressed as Jack.

" With care, perhaps."

" Will you be responsible for him, Jack Hamlin?" said the sheriff, suddenly.

" I will."

" Then take him. Stay, he 's coming to."

The wounded man slowly opened his eyes. They fell upon Jack Hamlin with a pleased look of recognition, but almost instantly and anxiously glanced around as if seeking another. Leaning over him, Jack said gayly, " They 've passed you over to me, old man; are you willing?"

The wounded man's eyes assented, but still moved restlessly from side to side.

" Is there any one you want to go with you?"

" Yes," said the eyes.

" The doctor, of course?"

The eyes did not answer. Gideon dropped
on his knees beside him. A ray of light
flashed in the helpless man's eyes and transfigured his whole face.

"You want *him?*" said Jack incredulously.

"Yes," said the eyes.

"What — the preacher?"

The lips struggled to speak. Everybody
bent down to hear his reply.

"You bet," he said faintly.

IV.

It was early morning when the wagon
containing the wounded man, Gideon, Jack
Hamlin, and the surgeon crept slowly through
the streets of Martinez and stopped before
the door of the "Palmetto Shades." The
upper floor of this saloon and hostelry was
occupied by Mr. Hamlin as his private lodgings, and was fitted up with the usual luxury and more than the usual fastidiousness
of his extravagant class. As the dusty and

travel-worn party trod the soft carpets and
brushed aside their silken hangings in their
slow progress with their helpless burden to
the lace-canopied and snowy couch of the
young gambler, it seemed almost a profana-
tion of some feminine seclusion.   Gideon,
to whom such luxury was unknown, was profoundly troubled.   The voluptuous ease and
sensuousness, the refinements of a life of
irresponsible indulgence, affected him with a
physical terror to which in his late moment
of real peril he had been a stranger; the
gilding and mirrors blinded his eyes; even
the faint perfume seemed to him an unhal-
lowed incense, and turned him sick and
giddy.   Accustomed as he had been to dis-
ease and misery in its humblest places and
meanest surroundings, the wounded despe-
rado lying in laces and fine linen seemed to
him monstrous and unnatural.   It required
all his self-abnegation, all his sense of duty,
all his deep pity, and all the instinctive tact
which was born of his gentle thoughtfulness

for others, to repress a shrinking. But when
the miserable cause of all again opened his
eyes and sought Gideon's hand, he forgot it
all. Happily, Hamlin, who had been watching him with wondering but critical eyes,
mistook his concern. "Don't you worry
about that gin - mill and hash - gymnasium
downstairs," he said. "I 've given the proprietor a thousand dollars to shut up shop as
long as this thing lasts." That this was done
from some delicate sense of respect to the
preacher's domiciliary presence, and not entirely to secure complete quiet and seclusion
for the invalid, was evident from the fact that
Mr. Hamlin's drawing and dining rooms, and
even the hall, were filled with eager friends
and inquirers. It was discomposing to Gideon to find himself almost an equal subject
of interest and curiosity to the visitors. The
story of his simple devotion had lost nothing by report ; hats were doffed in his presence that might have grown to their wearers'
heads ; the boldest eyes dropped as he passed

by; he had only to put his pale face out of the bedroom door and the loudest discussion, heated by drink or affection, fell to a whisper. The surgeon, who had recognized the one dominant wish of the hopelessly sinking man, gravely retired, leaving Gideon a few simple instructions and directions for their use. "He'll last as long as he has need of you," he said respectfully. "My art is only second here. God help you both! When he wakes, make the most of your time."

In a few moments he did waken, and as before turned his fading look almost instinctively on the faithful, gentle eyes that were watching him. How Gideon made the most of his time did not transpire, but at the end of an hour, when the dying man had again lapsed into unconsciousness, he softly opened the door of the sitting-room.

Hamlin started hastily to his feet. He had cleared the room of his visitors, and was alone. He turned a moment towards the window before he faced Gideon with inquiring but curiously-shining eyes.

" Well? " he said, hesitatingly.

" Do you know Kate Somers? " asked Gideon.

Hamlin opened his brown eyes.   " Yes."

" Can you send for her? "

" What, *here* ? "

" Yes, here."

" What for? "

" To marry him," said Gideon, gently. " There 's no time to lose."

" To *marry* him? "

" He wishes it."

" But say — oh, come, now," said Hamlin confidentially, leaning back with his hands on the top of a chair.   " Ain't this playing it a little — just a *little* — too low down? Of course you mean well, and all that; but come, now, say — could n't you just let up on him there?   Why, she " — Hamlin softly closed the door — " she 's got no character."

" The more reason he should give her one."

A cynical knowledge of matrimony imparted to him by the wives of others evidently colored Mr. Hamlin's views. "Well, perhaps it's all the same if he's going to die. But isn't it rather rough on *her?* I don't know," he added, reflectively; "she was sniveling round here a little while ago, until I sent her away."

"You sent her away!" echoed Gideon.

"I did."

"Why?"

"Because *you* were here."

Nevertheless Mr. Hamlin departed, and in half an hour reappeared with two brilliantly dressed women. One, hysterical, tearful, frightened, and pallid, was the destined bride; the other, highly colored, excited, and pleasedly observant, was her friend. Two men hastily summoned from the anteroom as witnesses completed the group that moved into the bedroom and gathered round the bed.

The ceremony was simple and brief. It was well, for of all who took part in it none

was more shaken by emotion than the offi-
ciating priest. The brilliant dresses of the
women, the contrast of their painted faces
with the waxen pallor of the dying man;
the terrible incongruity of their voices, in-
flections, expressions, and familiarity; the
mingled perfume of cosmetics and the faint
odor of wine; the eyes of the younger woman following his movements with strange
absorption, so affected him that he was glad
when he could fall on his knees at last and
bury his face in the pillow of the sufferer.
The hand that had been placed in the bride's
cold fingers slipped from them and mechanically sought Gideon's again. The significance of the unconscious act brought the first
spontaneous tears into the woman's eyes.
It was his last act, for when Gideon's voice
was again lifted in prayer, the spirit for
whom it was offered had risen with it, as it
were, still lovingly hand in hand, from the
earth forever.

The funeral was arranged for two days

later, and Gideon found that his services had been so seriously yet so humbly counted upon by the friends of the dead man that he could scarce find it in his heart to tell them that it was the function of the local preacher — an older and more experienced man than himself. "If it is," said Jack Hamlin, coolly, "I'm afraid he won't get a yaller dog to come to his church; but if you say you'll preach at the grave, there ain't a man, woman, or child that will be kept away. Don't you go back on your luck, now; it's something awful and nigger-like. You've got this crowd where the hair is short; excuse me, but it's so. Talk of revivals! You could give that one-horse show in Tasajara a hundred points, and skunk them easily." Indeed had Gideon been accessible to vanity, the spontaneous homage he met with everywhere would have touched him more sympathetically and kindly than it did; but in the utter unconsciousness of his own power and the quality they worshiped in him, he felt

alarmed and impatient of what he believed
to be their weak sympathy with his own human weakness. In the depth of his unselfish
heart, lit, it must be confessed, only by the
scant, inefficient lamp of his youthful experience, he really believed he had failed in his
apostolic mission because he had been unable to touch the hearts of the Vigilantes by
oral appeal and argument. Feeling thus, the
reverence of these irreligious people that
surrounded him, the facile yielding of their
habits and prejudices to his half - uttered
wish, appeared to him only a temptation of
the flesh. No one had sought him after the
manner of the camp-meeting; he had converted the wounded man through a common
weakness of their humanity. More than
that, he was. conscious of a growing fascination for the truthfulness and sincerity of
that class; particularly of Mr. Jack Hamlin, whose conversion he felt he could never
attempt, yet whose strange friendship alter-
nately thrilled and frightened him.

It was the evening before the funeral.
The coffin, half smothered in wreaths and
flowers, stood upon trestles in the anteroom;
a large silver plate bearing an inscription on
which for the second time Gideon read the
name of the man he had converted. It was
a name associated on the frontier so often
with reckless hardihood, dissipation, and
blood, that even now Gideon trembled at his
presumption, and was chilled by a momentary
doubt of the efficiency of his labor. Drawing unconsciously nearer to the mute subject of his thoughts, he threw his arms across
the coffin and buried his face between them.

A stream of soft music, the echo of some
forgotten song, seemed to Gideon to suddenly fill and possess the darkened room,
and then to slowly die away, like the opening
and shutting of a door upon a flood of golden
radiance. He listened with hushed breath
and a beating heart. He had never heard
anything like it before. Again the strain
arose, the chords swelled round him, until

from their midst a tenor voice broke high
and steadfast, like a star in troubled skies.
Gideon scarcely breathed. It was a hymn
— but such a hymn. He had never conceived there could be such beautiful words,
joined to such exquisite melody, and sung
with a grace so tender and true. What
were all other hymns to this ineffable yearn-
ing for light, for love, and for infinite rest?
Thrilled and exalted, Gideon felt his doubts
pierced and scattered by that illuminating
cry. Suddenly he rose, and with a troubled
thought pushed open the door to the sitting-
room. It was Mr. Jack Hamlin sitting before a parlor organ. The music ceased.

"It was *you*," stammered Gideon.

Jack nodded, struck a few chords by way
of finish, and then wheeled round on the
music-stool towards Gideon. His face was
slightly flushed. "Yes. I used to be the
organist and tenor in our church in the
States. I used to snatch the sinners bald-
headed with that. Do you know I reckon

I 'll sing that to-morrow, if you like, and maybe afterwards we 'll — but " — he stopped —
" we 'll talk of that after the funeral. It 's
business." Seeing Gideon still glancing with
a troubled air from the organ to himself,
he said : " Would you like to try that hymn
with me ? Come on ! "

He again struck the chords. As the whole
room seemed to throb with the music, Gideon
felt himself again carried away. Glancing
over Jack's shoulders, he could read the
words but not the notes ; yet, having a quick
ear for rhythm, he presently joined in with
a deep but uncultivated baritone. Together
they forgot everything else, and at the end of
an hour were only recalled by the presence
of a silently admiring concourse of votive-
offering friends who had gathered round
them.

The funeral took place the next day at the
grave dug in the public cemetery — a green
area fenced in by the palisading tules. The
words of Gideon were brief but humble ; the

strongest partisan of the dead man could find no fault in a confession of human frailty in which the speaker humbly confessed his share; and when the hymn was started by Hamlin and taken up by Gideon, the vast multitude, drawn by interest and curiosity, joined as in a solemn Amen.

Later, when those two strangely-assorted friends had returned to Mr. Hamlin's rooms previous to Gideon's departure, the former, in a manner more serious than his habitual cynical good-humor, began: " I said I had to talk business with you. The boys about here want to build a church for you, and are ready to plank the money down if you 'll say it 's a go. You understand they are n't asking you to run in opposition to that Gospel sharp — excuse me — that 's here now, nor do they want you to run a side show in connection with it. They want you to be independent. They don't pin you down to any kind of religion, you know; whatever you care to give them — Methodist, Roman

Catholic, Presbyterian — is mighty good enough for them, if you 'll expound it. You might give a little of each, or one on one day and one another — they 'll never know the difference if you only mix the drinks yourself. They 'll give you a house and guarantee you fifteen hundred dollars the first year."

He stopped and walked towards the window. The sunlight that fell upon his handsome face seemed to call back the careless smile to his lips and the reckless fire to his brown eyes. "I don't suppose there 's a man among them that would n't tell you all this in a great deal better way than I do. But the darned fools — excuse me — would have *me* break it to you. Why, I don't know. I need n't tell you I like you — not only for what you did for George — but I like you for your style — for yourself. And I want you to accept. You could keep these rooms till they got a house ready for you. Together — you and me — we 'd make that organ howl. But because I like it — because it's everything to us — and nothing to you, it don't seem square for me to ask it. Does it?"

Gideon replied by taking Hamlin's hand. His face was perfectly pale, but his look collected. He had not expected this offer, and yet when it was made he felt as if he had known it before — as if he had been warned of it — as if it was the great temptation of his life. Watching him with an earnestness only slightly overlaid by his usual manner, Hamlin went on.

" I know it would be lonely here, and a man like you ought to have a wife for " — he slightly lifted his eyebrows — " for example's sake. I heard there was a young lady in the case over there in Tasajara — but the old people did n't see it on account of your position. They'd jump at it now. Eh? No? Well," continued Jack, with a decent attempt to conceal his cynical relief, " perhaps those boys have been so eager to find

out all they could do for you that they've
been sold. Perhaps we're making equal
fools of ourselves now in asking you to stay.
But don't say no just yet — take a day or a
week to think of it."

Gideon still pale but calm, cast his eyes
around the elegant room, at the magic organ,
then upon the slight handsome figure before
him. " I *will* think of it," he said, in a low
voice, as he pressed Jack's hand. " And if
I accept you will find me here to-morrow
afternoon at this time ; if I do not you will
know that I keep with me wherever I go the
kindness, the brotherly love, and the grace
of God that prompts your offer, even though
He withholds from me His blessed light,
which alone can make me know His wish."
He stopped and hesitated. "If you love
me, Jack, don't ask me to stay, but pray for
that light which alone can guide my feet
back to you, or take me hence for ever."
He once more tightly pressed the hand of
the embarrassed man before him and was
gone.

Passers-by on the Martinez road that night remembered a mute and ghostly rider who, heedless of hail or greeting, moved by them as in a trance or vision. But the Widow Hiler the next morning, coming from the spring, found no abstraction or preoccupation in the soft eyes of Gideon Deane as he suddenly appeared before her, and gently relieved her of the bucket she was carrying. A quick flush of color over her brow and cheek-bone, as if a hot iron had passed there, and a certain astringent coyness, would have embarrassed any other man than him.

"Sho, it's *you*. I reck'ned I'd seen the last of you."

"You don't mean that, Sister Hiler?" said Gideon, with a gentle smile.

"Well, what with the report of your goin's on at Martinez and improvin' the occasion of that sinner's death, and leadin' a revival, I reckoned you'ld hev forgotten low folks at Tasajara. And if your goin' to be settled there in a new church, with new hearers, I reckon you'll want new surroundings too. Things change and young folks change with 'em."

They had reached the house. Her breath was quick and short as if she and not Gideon had borne the burden. He placed the bucket in its accustomed place, and then gently took her hand in his. The act precipitated the last drop of feeble coquetry she had retained, and the old tears took its place. Let us hope for the last time. For as Gideon stooped and lifted her ailing babe in his strong arms, he said softly, " Whatever God has wrought for me since we parted, I know now He has called me to but one work."

" And that work? " she asked, tremulously.

" To watch over the widow and fatherless. And with God's blessing, sister, and His holy ordinance, I am here to stay."

SARAH WALKER.

It was very hot. Not a breath of air was stirring throughout the western wing of the Greyport Hotel, and the usual feverish life of its four hundred inmates had succumbed to the weather. The great veranda was deserted; the corridors were desolated; no footfall echoed in the passages; the lazy rustle of a wandering skirt, or a passing sigh that was half a pant, seemed to intensify the heated silence. An intoxicated bee, disgracefully unsteady in wing and leg, who had been holding an inebriated conversation with himself in the corner of my window pane, had gone to sleep at last and was snoring. The errant prince might have entered the slumberous halls unchallenged, and walked into any of the darkened rooms whose open doors gaped for more air, without awakening the veriest Greyport flirt with his salutation. At times a drowsy voice, a lazily interjected sentence, an incoherent protest, a long-drawn phrase of saccharine tenuity suddenly broken off with a gasp, came vaguely to the ear, as if indicating a half-suspended, half-articulated existence somewhere, but not definite enough to indicate conversation. In the midst of this, there was the sudden crying of a child.

I looked up from my work. Through the camera of my jealously guarded window, I could catch a glimpse of the vivid, quivering blue of the sky, the glittering intensity of the ocean, the long motionless leaves of the horse-chestnut in the road, — all utterly inconsistent with anything as active as this lamentation. I stepped to the open door and into the silent hall.

Apparently the noise had attracted the equal attention of my neighbors. A vague chorus of "Sarah Walker," in querulous recognition, of "O Lord! that child again!" in hopeless protest, rose faintly from the different rooms. As the lamentations seemed to approach nearer, the visitors' doors were successively shut, swift footsteps hurried along the hall; past my open door came a momentary vision of a heated nursemaid carrying a tumultuous chaos of frilled skirts, flying sash, rebellious slippers, and tossing curls; there was a moment's rallying struggle before the room nearly opposite mine, and then a door opened and shut upon the vision. It was Sarah Walker!

Everybody knew her; few had ever seen more of her than this passing vision. In the great hall, in the dining-room, in the vast parlors, in the garden, in the avenue, on the beach, a sound of lamentation had always been followed by this same brief apparition. Was there a sudden pause among the dancers and a subjugation of the loudest bassoons in the early evening "hop," the ex-

planation was given in the words " Sarah
Walker." Was there a wild confusion
among the morning bathers on the sands,
people whispered " Sarah Walker." A panic
among the waiters at dinner, an interruption
in the Sunday sacred concert, a disorgani-
zation of the after-dinner promenade on the
veranda, was instantly referred to Sarah
Walker. Nor were her efforts confined entirely to public life. In cozy corners and
darkened recesses, bearded lips withheld
the amorous declaration to mutter " Sarah
Walker " between their clenched teeth; coy
and bashful tongues found speech at last in
the rapid formulation of " Sarah Walker."
Nobody ever thought of abbreviating her
full name. The two people in the hotel,
otherwise individualized, but known only
as " Sarah Walker's father " and " Sarah
Walker's mother," and never as Mr. and
Mrs. Walker, addressed her only as " Sarah
Walker;" two animals that were occasionally a part of this passing pageant were

known as "Sarah Walker's dog" and "Sarah Walker's cat," and later it was my proud privilege to sink my own individuality under the title of "that friend of Sarah Walker's."

It must not be supposed that she had attained this baleful eminence without some active criticism. Every parent in the Greyport Hotel had held his or her theory of the particular defects of Sarah Walker's education; every virgin and bachelor had openly expressed views of the peculiar discipline that was necessary to her subjugation. It may be roughly estimated that she would have spent the entire nine years of her active life in a dark cupboard on an exclusive diet of bread and water, had this discipline obtained; while, on the other hand, had the educational theories of the parental assembly prevailed, she would have ere this shone an etherealized essence in the angelic host. In either event she would have "ceased from troubling," which was the general Greyport idea of higher education. A paper read before our Literary Society on " Sarah-Walker and other infantile diseases," was referred to in the catalogue as " Walker, Sarah, Prevention and Cure," while the usual burlesque legislation of our summer season culminated in the Act entitled " An Act to amend an Act entitled an Act for the abatement of Sarah Walker." As she was hereafter exclusively to be fed " on the *provisions* of this Act," some idea of its general tone may be gathered. It was a singular fact in this point of her history that her natural progenitors not only offered no resistance to the doubtful celebrity of their offspring, but, by hopelessly accepting the situation, to some extent *posed* as Sarah Walker's victims. Mr. and Mrs. Walker were known to be rich, respectable, and indulgent to their only child. They themselves had been evolved from a previous generation of promiscuously acquired wealth into the repose of inherited property, but it was currently accepted that Sarah had " cast back " and reincarnated

some waif on the deck of an emigrant ship
at the beginning of the century.

Such was the child separated from me by
this portentous history, a narrow passage,
and a closed nursery door. Presently, however, the door was partly opened again as if
to admit the air. The crying had ceased,
but in its place the monotonous Voice of
Conscience, for the moment personated by
Sarah Walker's nursemaid, kept alive a
drowsy recollection of Sarah Walker's trans-
gressions.

" You see," said the Voice, " what a dreadful thing it is for a little girl to go on as you
do. I am astonished at you, Sarah Walker.
So is everybody; so is the good ladies next
door ; so is the kind gentleman opposite ; so
is all ! Where you expect to go to, 'Evin
only knows ! How you expect to be forgiven,
saints alone can tell ! But so it is always,
and yet you keep it up. And would n't you
like it different, Sarah Walker ? Would n't
you like to have everybody love you ?

Would n't you like them good ladies next door, and that nice gentleman opposite, all to kinder rise up and say, ' Oh, what a dear good little girl Sarah Walker is?'" The interpolation of a smacking sound of lips, as if in unctuous anticipation of Sarah Walker's virtue, here ensued — " Oh, what a dear, good, sw-e-et, lovely little girl Sarah Walker is!"

There was a dead silence. It may have been fancy, but I thought that some of the doors in the passage creaked softly as if in listening expectation. Then the silence was broken by a sigh. Had Sarah Walker ingloriously succumbed? Rash and impotent conclusion!

" I don't," said Sarah Walker's voice, slowly rising until it broke on the crest of a mountainous sob, " I — don't — want — 'em — to — love me. I — don't want — 'em — to say — what a — dear — good — little girl — Sarah Walker is!" She caught her breath. " I — want — 'em — to say — what

a naughty — bad — dirty — horrid — filthy
— little girl Sarah Walker is — so I do.
There! ''

The doors slammed all along the passages.
The dreadful issue was joined. I softly
crossed the hall and looked into Sarah
Walker's room.

The light from a half-opened shutter fell
full upon her rebellious little figure. She
had stiffened herself in a large easy-chair
into the attitude in which she had been evidently deposited there by the nurse whose
torn-off apron she still held rigidly in one
hand. Her shapely legs stood out before
her, jointless and inflexible to the point of
her tiny shoes — a *pose* copied with pathetic
fidelity by the French doll at her feet. The
attitude must have been dreadfully uncomfortable, and maintained only as being re-
plete with some vague insults to the person
who had put her down, as exhibiting a wild
indecorum of silken stocking. A mystified
kitten — Sarah Walker's inseparable — was

held as rigidly under one arm with equal
dumb aggressiveness. Following the stiff
line of her half-recumbent figure, her head
suddenly appeared perpendicularly erect —
yet the only mobile part of her body. A
dazzling sunburst of silky hair, the color of
burnished copper, partly hid her neck and
shoulders and the back of the chair. Her
eyes were a darker shade of the same color
— the orbits appearing deeper and larger
from the rubbing in of habitual tears from
long wet lashes. Nothing so far seemed inconsistent with her infelix reputation, but,
strange to say, her other features were
marked by delicacy and refinement, and her
mouth — that sorely exercised and justly
dreaded member — was small and pretty,
albeit slightly dropped at the corners.

The immediate effect of my intrusion was
limited solely to the nursemaid. Swooping
suddenly upon Sarah Walker's too evident
déshabillé, she made two or three attempts
to pluck her into propriety ; but the child,

recognizing the cause as well as the effect, looked askance at me and only stiffened herself the more. " Sarah Walker, I 'm shocked."

" It ain't *his* room anyway," said Sarah, eying me malevolently. " What 's he doing here ? "

There was so much truth in this that I involuntarily drew back abashed. The nurse-maid ejaculated " Sarah ! " and lifted her eyes in hopeless protest.

" And he need n't come seeing *you*," continued Sarah, lazily rubbing the back of her head against the chair ; " my papa don't allow it. He warned you 'bout the other gentleman, you know."

" Sarah Walker ! "

I felt it was necessary to say something. " Don't you want to come with me and look at the sea ? " I said with utter feebleness of invention. To my surprise, instead of actively assaulting me Sarah Walker got up, shook her hair over her shoulders, and took my hand.

"With your hair in that state?" almost screamed the domestic. But Sarah Walker had already pulled me into the hall. What particularly offensive form of opposition to authority was implied in this prompt assent to my proposal I could only darkly guess. For myself I knew I must appear to her a weak impostor. What would there possibly be in the sea to interest Sarah Walker? For the moment I prayed for a water-spout, a shipwreck, a whale, or any marine miracle to astound her and redeem my character. I walked guiltily down the hall, holding her hand bashfully in mine. I noticed that her breast began to heave convulsively; if she cried I knew I should mingle my tears with hers. We reached the veranda in gloomy silence. As I expected, the sea lay before us glittering in the sun — vacant, staring, flat, and hopelessly and unquestionably uninteresting.

"I knew it all along," said Sarah Walker, turning down the corners of her mouth;

" there never was anything to see. I know why you got me to come here. You want to tell me if I 'm a good girl you 'll take me to sail some day. You want to say if I 'm bad the sea will swallow me up. That's all you want, you horrid thing you ! "

" Hush ! " I said, pointing to the corner of the veranda.

A desperate idea of escape had just seized me. Bolt upright in the recess of a window sat a nursemaid who had succumbed to sleep equally with her helpless charge in the perambulator beside her. I instantly recognized the infant — a popular organism known as " Baby Buckly " — the prodigy of the Greyport Hotel, the pet of its enthusiastic womanhood. Fat and featureless, pink and pincushiony, it was borrowed by gushing maidenhood, exchanged by idiotic maternity, and had grown unctuous and tumefacient under the kisses and embraces of half the hotel. Even in its present repose it looked moist and shiny from indiscriminate and promiscuous osculation.

" Let 's borrow Baby Buckly," I said reck-
lessly.

Sarah Walker at once stopped crying.   I
don't know how she did it, but the cessation
was instantaneous, as if she had turned off
a tap somewhere.

"And put it in Mr. Peters' bed!" I continued.

Peters being notoriously a grim bachelor,
the bare suggestion bristled with outrage.
Sarah Walker's eyes sparkled.

" You don't mean it! — go 'way!" — she
said with affected coyness.

" But I do!   Come."

We extracted it noiselessly together —
that is, Sarah Walker did, with deft woman-
liness — carried it darkly along the hall to
No. 27, and deposited it in Peters' bed, where
it lay like a freshly opened oyster. We then
returned hand in hand to my room, where
we looked out of the window on the sea.   It
was observable that there was no lack of interest in Sarah Walker now.

Before five minutes had elapsed some one breathlessly passed the open door while we were still engaged in marine observation. This was followed by return footsteps and a succession of swiftly rustling garments, until the majority of the women in our wing had apparently passed our room, and we saw an irregular stream of nursemaids and mothers converging towards the hotel out of the grateful shadow of arbors, trees, and marquees. In fact we were still engaged in observation when Sarah Walker's nurse came to fetch her away, and to inform her that " by rights " Baby Buckly's nurse and Mr. Peters should both be made to leave the hotel that very night. Sarah Walker permitted herself to be led off with dry but expressive eyes. That evening she did not cry, but, on being taken into the usual custody for disturbance, was found to be purple with suppressed laughter.

This was the beginning of my intimacy with Sarah Walker. But while it was evident that whatever influence I obtained over

her was due to my being *particeps criminis,*
I think it was accepted that a regular abduc-
tion of infants might become in time monotonous if not dangerous. So she was satisfied
with the knowledge that I could not now,
without the most glaring hypocrisy, obtrude
a moral superiority upon her. I do not think
she would have turned state evidence and
accused me, but I was by no means assured
of her disinterested regard. She contented
herself, for a few days afterwards, with meeting me privately and mysteriously communicating unctuous reminiscences of our joint
crime, without suggesting a repetition. Her
intimacy with me did not seem to interfere
with her general relations to her own species
in the other children in the hotel. Perhaps
I should have said before that her popularity
with them was by no means prejudiced by
her infelix reputation. But while she was
secretly admired by all, she had few professed
followers and no regular associates. Whether
the few whom she selected for that baleful

preëminence were either torn from her by horrified guardians, or came to grief through her dangerous counsels, or whether she really did not care for them, I could not say. Their elevation was brief, their retirement unregretted. It was however permitted me, through felicitous circumstances, to become acquainted with the probable explanation of her unsociability.

The very hot weather culminated one afternoon in a dead faint of earth and sea and sky. An Alpine cloudland of snow that had mocked the upturned eyes of Greyport for hours, began to darken under the folding shadow of a black and velvety wing. The atmosphere seemed to thicken as the gloom increased ; the lazy dust, thrown up by hurrying feet that sought a refuge, hung almost motionless in the air. Suddenly it was blown to the four quarters in one fierce gust that as quickly dispersed the loungers drooping in shade and cover. For a few seconds the long avenue was lost in flying clouds of dust, and then was left bare of life or motion. Raindrops in huge stars and rosettes appeared noiselessly and magically upon the sidewalks — gouts of moisture apparently dropped from mid-air. And then the ominous hush returned.

A mile away along the rocks, I turned for shelter into a cavernous passage of the overhanging cliff, where I could still watch the coming storm upon the sea. A murmur of voices presently attracted my attention. I then observed that the passage ended in a kind of open grotto, where I could dimly discern the little figures of several children, who, separated from their nurses in the sudden onset of the storm, had taken refuge there. As the gloom deepened they became silent again, until the stillness was broken by a familiar voice. There was no mistaking it. — It was Sarah Walker's. But it was not lifted in lamentation, it was raised only as if resuming a suspended narrative.

" Her name," said Sarah Walker gloomily,

" was Kribbles. She was the only child —
of — of orphaned parentage, and fair to see,
but she was bad, and God did not love her.
And one day she was separated from her
nurse on a desert island like to this. And
then came a hidgeous thunderstorm. And
a great big thunderbolt came galumping
after her. And it ketched her and rolled all
over her — so! and then it came back and
ketched her and rolled her over — so! And
when they came to pick her up there was not
so much as *that* left of her. All burnt up! "

" Was n't there just a little bit of her
shoe? " suggested a cautious auditor.

"Not a bit," said Sarah Walker firmly.
All the other children echoed " Not a bit,"
indignantly, in evident gratification at the
completeness of Kribbles' catastrophe. At
this moment the surrounding darkness was
suddenly filled with a burst of blue celes-
tial fire; the heavy inky sea beyond, the
black-edged mourning horizon, the gleaming
sands, each nook and corner of the dripping

cave, with the frightened faces of the huddled group of children, started into vivid life for an instant, and then fell back with a deafening crash into the darkness.

There was a slight sound of whimpering. Sarah Walker apparently pounced upon the culprit, for it ceased.

" Sniffling 'tracts 'lectricity," she said sententiously.

" But you thaid it wath Dod ! " lisped a casuist of seven.

" It 's all the same," said Sarah sharply, " and so 's asking questions."

This obscure statement was however apparently understood, for the casuist lapsed into silent security.   " Lots of things 'tracts it," continued Sarah Walker.   " Gold and silver, and metals and knives and rings."

" And pennies ? "

" And pennies most of all !   Kribbles was that vain, she used to wear jewelry and fly in the face of Providence."

" But you thaid " —

" Will you ? — There ! you hear that ? "
There was another blinding flash and bound-
ing roll of thunder along the shore. " I
wonder you did n't ketch it. You would —
only I 'm here."

All was quiet again, but from certain indications it was evident that a collection of
those dangerous articles that had proved
fatal to the unhappy Kribbles was being
taken up. I could hear the clink of coins
and jingle of ornaments. That Sarah herself was the custodian was presently shown.
" But won't the lightning come to you now ? "
asked a timid voice.

" No," said Sarah, promptly, " 'cause I
ain't afraid ! Look ! "

A frightened protest from the children
here ensued, but the next instant she appeared at the entrance of the grotto and ran
down the rocks towards the sea. Skipping
from bowlder to bowlder she reached the
furthest projection of the ledge, now partly
submerged by the rising surf, and then

6

turned half triumphantly, half defiantly, towards the grotto. The weird phosphorescence of the storm lit up the resolute little figure standing there, gorgeously bedecked with the chains, rings, and shiny trinkets of her companions. With a tiny hand raised in mock defiance of the elements, she seemed to lean confidingly against the panting breast of the gale, with fluttering skirt and flying tresses. Then the vault behind her cracked with three jagged burning fissures, a weird flame leaped upon the sand, there was a cry of terror from the grotto, echoed by a scream of nurses on the cliff, a deluge of rain, a terrific onset from the gale — and — Sarah Walker was gone? Nothing of the kind! When I reached the ledge, after a severe struggle with the storm, I found Sarah on the leeward side, drenched but delighted. I held her tightly, while we waited for a lull to regain the cliff, and took advantage of the sympathetic situation.

"But you know you *were* frightened,

Sarah," I whispered; "you thought of what happened to poor Kribbles."

" Do you know who Kribbles was ? " she asked confidentially.

" No."

" Well," she whispered, " I made Kribbles up. And the hidgeous storm and thunderbolt — and the burning ! All out of my own head."

The only immediate effect of this escapade was apparently to precipitate and bring into notoriety the growing affection of an obscure lover of Sarah Walker's, hitherto unsuspected. He was a mild inoffensive boy of twelve, known as " Warts," solely from an inordinate exhibition of these youthful excrescences. On the day of Sarah Walker's adventure his passion culminated in a sudden and illogical attack upon Sarah's nurse and parents while they were bewailing her conduct, and in assaulting them with his feet and hands. Whether he associated them in some vague way with the cause of her momentary peril, or whether he only wished to impress her with the touching flattery of a general imitation of her style, I cannot say. For his love-making was peculiar. A day or two afterwards he came to my open door and remained for some moments bashfully looking at me. The next day I found him standing by my chair in the piazza with an embarrassed air and in utter inability to explain his conduct. At the end of a rapid walk on the sand one morning, I was startled by the sound of hurried breath, and looking around, discovered the staggering Warts quite exhausted by endeavoring to keep up with me on his short legs. At last the daily recurrence of his haunting presence forced a dreadful suspicion upon me. Warts was courting *me* for Sarah Walker! Yet it was impossible to actually connect her with these mute attentions. "You want me to give them to Sarah Walker," I said cheerfully one afternoon, as he laid upon my desk some peculiarly uninviting crustacea which looked

not unlike a few detached excrescences from
his own hands. He shook his head decid-
edly. "I understand," I continued, con-
fidently; "you want me to keep them for
her." "No," said Warts, doggedly. "Then
you only want me to tell her how nice they
are?" The idea was apparently so shame-
lessly true that he blushed himself hastily
into the passage, and ceased any future con-
tribution. Naturally still more ineffective
was the slightest attempt to bring his devotion into the physical presence of Sarah
Walker. The most ingenious schemes to lure
him into my room while she was there failed
utterly. Yet he must have at one time
basked in her baleful presence. "Do you
like Warts?" I asked her one day bluntly.
"Yes," said Sarah Walker with cheerful
directness; "ain't *he* got a lot of 'em? —
though he used to have more. But," she
added reflectively, "do you know the little
Ilsey boy?" I was compelled to admit my
ignorance. "Well!" she said with a rem-

iniscent sigh of satisfaction, " *he 's* got only
two toes on his left foot — showed 'em to
me. And he was born so." Need it be
said that in these few words I read the dis-
mal sequel of Warts' unfortunate attach-
ment? His accidental eccentricity was no
longer attractive. What were his evanescent
accretions, subject to improvement or removal, beside the hereditary and settled mal-
formations of his rival?

Once only, in this brief summer episode,
did Sarah Walker attract the impulsive and
general sympathy of Greyport. It is only
just to her consistency to say it was through
no fault of hers, unless a characteristic ex-
posure which brought on a chill and diphthe-
ria could be called her own act. Howbeit,
towards the close of the season, when a sudden suggestion of the coming autumn had
crept, one knew not how, into the heart of a
perfect day ; when even a return of the summer warmth had a suspicion of hectic, — on
one of these days Sarah Walker was missed

with the bees and the butterflies. For two days her voice had not been heard in hall or corridor, nor had the sunshine of her French marigold head lit up her familiar places. The two days were days of relief, yet mitigated with a certain uneasy apprehension of the return of Sarah Walker, or — more alarming thought! — the Sarah Walker element in a more appalling form. So strong was this impression that an unhappy infant who unwittingly broke this interval with his maiden outcry was nearly lynched. "We 're not going to stand that from *you*, you know," was the crystallized sentiment of a brutal bachelor. In fact, it began to be admitted that Greyport had been accustomed to Sarah Walker's ways. In the midst of this, it was suddenly whispered that Sarah Walker was lying dangerously ill, and was not expected to live.

Then occurred one of those strange revulsions of human sentiment which at first seem to point the dawning of a millennium of poetic justice, but which, in this case, ended in merely stirring the languid pulses of society into a hectic fever, and in making sympathy for Sarah Walker an insincere and exaggerated fashion. Morning and afternoon visits to her apartment, with extravagant offerings, were *de rigueur;* bulletins were issued three times a day; an allusion to her condition was the recognized preliminary to all conversation; advice, suggestions, and petitions to restore the baleful existence flowed readily from the same facile invention that had once proposed its banishment; until one afternoon the shadow had drawn so close that even Folly withheld its careless feet before it, and laid down its feeble tinkling bells and gaudy cap tremblingly on the threshold. But the sequel must be told in more vivid words than mine.

"Whin I saw that angel lyin' there," said Sarah Walker's nurse, "as white, if ye plaze, as if the whole blessed blood of her body had gone to make up the beautiful glory of her hair; speechless as she was, I thought I saw a sort of longin' in her eyes.

" ' Is it anythin' you 'll be wantin', Sarah darlint,' sez her mother with a thremblin' voice, ' afore it 's lavin' us ye are? Is it the ministher yer askin' for, love? ' sez she.

" And Sarah looked at me, and if it was the last words I spake, her lips moved and she whispered ' Scotty.'

" ' Wirra! wirra! ' sez the mother, ' it 's wanderin' she is, the darlin'; ' for Scotty, don't ye see, was the grand bar-keeper of the hotel.

" ' Savin' yer presence, ma'am,' sez I, ' and the child's here, ez is half a saint already, it 's thruth she 's spakin' — it 's Scotty she wants.' And with that my angel blinks wid her black eyes ' yes.'

" ' Bring him,' says the docthor, ' at once.'

" And they bring him in wid all the mustachios and moighty fine curls of him, and his diamonds, rings, and pins all a-glistening just like his eyes when he set 'em on that suffering saint.

" ' Is it anythin' you 're wantin', Sarah dear ? ' sez he, thryin' to spake firm. And Sarah looks at him, and then looks at a tumbler on the table.

" 'Is it a bit of a cocktail, the likes of the one I made for ye last Sunday unbeknownst?' sez he, looking round mortal afraid of the parents. And Sarah Walker's eyes said, ' It is.' Then the ministher groaned, but the docthor jumps to his feet.

" ' Bring it,' sez he, ' and howld your jaw, an ye 's a Christian sowl.' And he brought it. An' afther the first sip, the child lifts herself up on one arm, and sez, with a swate smile and a toss of the glass :

" ' I looks towards you, Scotty,' sez she.

" ' I observes you and bows, miss,' sez he, makin' as if he was dhrinkin' wid her.

" ' Here 's another nail in yer coffin, old man,' sez she winkin'.

" ' And here 's the hair all off your head, miss,' sez he quite aisily, tossin' back the joke betwixt 'em.

" And with that she dhrinks it off, and lies down and goes to sleep like a lamb, and wakes up wid de rosy dawn in her cheeks, and the morthal seekness gone forever."

. . . .

Thus Sarah Walker recovered. Whether the fact were essential to the moral conveyed in these pages, I leave the reader to judge.

I was leaning on the terrace of the Kronprinzen-Hof at Rolandseck one hot summer afternoon, lazily watching the groups of tourists strolling along the road that ran between the Hof and the Rhine. There was certainly little in the place or its atmosphere to recall the Greyport episode of twenty years before, when I was suddenly startled by hearing the name of "Sarah Walker."

In the road below me were three figures, — a lady, a gentleman, and a little girl. As the latter turned towards the lady who addressed her, I recognized the unmistakable copper - colored tresses, trim figure, delicate complexion, and refined features of the

friend of my youth! I seized my hat, but
by the time I had reached the road, they
had disappeared.

The utter impossibility of its being Sarah
Walker herself, and the glaring fact that
the very coincidence of name would be inconsistent with any conventional descent
from the original Sarah, I admit confused
me. But I examined the book of the Kronprinzen-Hof and the other hotels, and ques-
tioned my *portier.* There was no "Mees"
nor "Madame Walkiere" extant in Rolandseck. Yet might not Monsieur have heard
incorrectly? The Czara Walka was evidently Russian, and Rolandseck was a resort for Russian princes. But pardon!
Did Monsieur really mean the young demoi-
selle now approaching? Ah! that was a different affair. She was the daughter of the
Italian Prince and Princess Monte Castello
staying here. The lady with her was not the
Princess, but a foreign friend. The gentleman was the Prince. Would he present
Monsieur's card?

They were entering the hotel. The Prince was a little, inoffensive-looking man, the lady an evident countrywoman of my own, and the child — was, yet was *not*, Sarah! There was the face, the outline, the figure — but the life, the verve, the audacity, was wanting! I could contain myself no longer.

"Pardon an inquisitive compatriot, madam," I said; "but I heard you a few moments ago address this young lady by the name of a very dear young friend, whom I knew twenty years ago — Sarah Walker. Am I right?"

The Prince stopped and gazed at us both with evident affright; then suddenly recognizing in my freedom some wild American indecorum, doubtless provoked by the presence of another of my species, which he really was not expected to countenance, retreated behind the *portier*. The circumstance by no means increased the good-will of the lady, as she replied somewhat haughtily: —

" The Principessina is named Sarah Walker, after her mother's maiden name."

" Then this *is* Sarah Walker's daughter ! " I said joyfully.

" She is the daughter of the Prince and Princess of Monte Castello," corrected the lady frigidly.

" I had the pleasure of knowing her mother very well." I stopped and blushed. Did I really know Sarah Walker very well? And would Sarah Walker know me now? Or would it not be very like her to go back on me? There was certainly anything but promise in the feeble-minded, vacuous copy of Sarah before me. I was yet hesitating, when the Prince, who had possibly received some quieting assurance from the *portier*, himself stepped forward, stammered that the Princess would, without doubt, be charmed to receive me later, and skipped upstairs, leaving the impression on my mind that he contemplated ordering his bill at once. There was no excuse for further prolonging the interview. " Say good-by to the strange gentleman, Sarah," suggested Sarah's companion stiffly. I looked at the child in the wild hope of recognizing some prompt resistance to the suggestion that would have identified her with the lost Sarah of my youth — but in vain. " Good-by, sir," said the affected little creature, dropping a mechanical curtsey. " Thank you very much for remembering my mother." " Good-by, Sarah!" It was indeed good-by forever.

For on my way to my room I came suddenly upon the Prince, in a recess of the upper hall, addressing somebody through an open door with a querulous protest, whose wild extravagance of statement was grotesquely balanced by its utter feeble timidity of manner. "It is," said the Prince, " indeed a grave affair. We have here hundreds of socialists, emissaries from lawless countries and impossible places, who travel thousands of miles to fall upon our hearts and embrace us. They establish an espionage over us ; they haunt our walks in incredible numbers ; they hang in droves upon our footsteps ; Heaven alone saves us from a public osculation at any moment ! They openly allege that they have dandled us on their knees at recent periods ; washed and dressed us, and would do so still. Our happiness, our security " —

"Don't be a fool, Prince. Do shut up ! "

The Prince collapsed and shrank away, and I hurried past the open door. A tall, magnificent-looking woman was standing before a glass, arranging her heavy red hair. The face, which had been impatiently turned towards the door, had changed again to profile, with a frown still visible on the bent brow. Our eyes met as I passed. The next moment the door slammed, and I had seen the last of Sarah Walker.

A SHIP OF '49.

It had rained so persistently in San Francisco during the first week of January, 1854, that a certain quagmire in the roadway of Long Wharf had become impassable, and a plank was thrown over its dangerous depth. Indeed, so treacherous was the spot that it was alleged, on good authority, that a hastily embarking traveler had once hopelessly lost his portmanteau, and was fain to dispose of his entire interest in it for the sum of two dollars and fifty cents to a speculative stranger on the wharf. As the stranger's search was rewarded afterwards only by the discovery of the body of a casual Chinaman, who had evidently endeavored wickedly to anticipate him, a feeling of com-

7

mercial insecurity was added to the other ec-
centricities of the locality.

The plank led to the door of a building
that was a marvel even in the chaotic frontier architecture of the street. The houses
on either side — irregular frames of wood or
corrugated iron — bore evidence of having
been quickly thrown together, to meet the
requirements of the goods and passengers
who were once disembarked on what was the
muddy beach of the infant city. But the
building in question exhibited a certain elab-
oration of form and design utterly inconsistent with this idea. The structure obtruded
a bowed front to the street, with a curving
line of small windows, surmounted by elaborate carvings and scroll work of vines and
leaves, while below, in faded gilt letters, appeared the legend " Pontiac — Marseilles."
The effect of this incongruity was startling.
It is related that an inebriated miner, im-
peded by mud and drink before its door,
was found gazing at its remarkable façade

with an expression of the deepest despondency. "I hev lived a free life, pardner," he explained thickly to the Samaritan who succored him, "and every time since I've been on this six weeks' jamboree might have kalkilated it would come to this. Snakes I've seen afore now, and rats I'm not unfamiliar with, but when it comes to the starn of a ship risin' up out of the street, I reckon it's time to pass in my checks." "It *is* a ship, you blasted old soaker," said the Samaritan curtly.

It was indeed a ship. A ship run ashore and abandoned on the beach years before by her gold-seeking crew, with the *débris* of her scattered stores and cargo, overtaken by the wild growth of the strange city and the reclamation of the muddy flat, wherein she lay hopelessly imbedded ; her retreat cut off by wharves and quays and breakwater, jostled at first by sheds, and then impacted in a block of solid warehouses and dwellings, her rudder, port, and counter boarded in, and now gazing hopelessly through her cabin windows upon the busy street before her. But still a ship despite her transformation. The faintest line of contour yet left visible spoke of the buoyancy of another element; the balustrade of her roof was unmistakably a taffrail. The rain slipped from her swelling sides with a certain lingering touch of the sea; the soil around her was still treacherous with its suggestions, and even the wind whistled nautically over her chimney. If, in the fury of some southwesterly gale, she had one night slipped her strange moorings and left a shining track through the lower town to the distant sea, no one would have been surprised.

Least of all, perhaps, her present owner and possessor, Mr. Abner Nott. For by the irony of circumstances, Mr. Nott was a Far Western farmer who had never seen a ship before, nor a larger stream of water than a tributary of the Missouri River. In a spirit, half of fascination, half of speculation, he

had bought her at the time of her abandon-
ment, and had since mortgaged his ranch at
Petaluma with his live stock, to defray the
expenses of filling in the land where she
stood, and the improvements of the vicinity.
He had transferred his household goods and
his only daughter to her cabin, and had divided the space " between decks " and her
hold into lodging-rooms, and lofts for the
storage of goods. It could hardly be said
that the investment had been profitable.
His tenants vaguely recognized that his oc-
cupancy was a sentimental rather than a
commercial speculation, and often generously
lent themselves to the illusion by not paying
their rent. Others treated their own ten-
ancy as a joke, — a quaint recreation born
of the childlike familiarity of frontier inter-
course. A few had left; carelessly aban-
doning their unsalable goods to their landlord, with great cheerfulness and a sense of
favor. Occasionally Mr. Abner Nott, in a
practical relapse, raged against the derelicts,

and talked of dispossessing them, or even dismantling his tenement, but he was easily placated by a compliment to the " dear old ship," or an effort made by some tenant to idealize his apartment. A photographer who had ingeniously utilized the forecastle for a gallery (accessible from the bows in the next street), paid no further tribute than a portrait of the pretty face of Rosey Nott. The superstitious reverence in which Abner Nott held his monstrous fancy was naturally enhanced by his purely bucolic exaggeration of its real functions and its native element. "This yer keel has sailed, and sailed, and sailed," he would explain with some incongruity of illustration, " in a bee line, makin' tracks for days runnin'. I reckon more storms and blizzards hez tackled her then you ken shake a stick at. She's stampeded whales afore now, and sloshed round with pirates and freebooters in and outer the Spanish Main, and across lots from Marcelleys where she was rared. And yer she sits

peaceful-like just ez if she 'd never been
outer a pertater patch, and had n't ploughed
the sea with fo'sails and studdin' sails and
them things cavortin' round her masts."

Abner Nott's enthusiasm was shared by
his daughter, but with more imagination, and
an intelligence stimulated by the scant lit-
erature of her father's emigrant wagon and
the few books found on the cabin shelves.
But to her the strange shell she inhabited
suggested more of the great world than the
rude, chaotic civilization she saw from the
cabin windows or met in the persons of her
father's lodgers. Shut up for days in this
quaint tenement, she had seen it change from
the enchanted playground of her childish
fancy to the theatre of her active maidenhood, but without losing her ideal romance
in it. She had translated its history in her
own way, read its quaint nautical hiero-
glyphics after her own fashion, and possessed herself of its secrets. She had in
fancy made voyages in it to foreign lands,

had heard the accents of a softer tongue on its decks, and on summer nights, from the roof of the quarter-deck, had seen mellower constellations take the place of the hard metallic glitter of the Californian skies. Sometimes, in her isolation, the long, cylindrical vault she inhabited seemed, like some vast sea-shell, to become musical with the murmurings of the distant sea. So completely had it taken the place of the usual instincts of feminine youth that she had forgotten she was pretty, or that her dresses were old in fashion and scant in quantity. After the first surprise of admiration her father's lodgers ceased to follow the abstracted nymph except with their eyes, — partly respecting her spiritual shyness, partly respecting the jealous supervision of the paternal Nott. She seldom penetrated the crowded centre of the growing city; her rare excursions were confined to the old ranch at Petaluma, whence she brought flowers and plants, and even extemporized a hanging-garden on the quarter-deck.

It was still raining, and the wind, which had increased to a gale, was dashing the drops against the slanting cabin windows with a sound like spray when Mr. Abner Nott sat before a table seriously engaged with his accounts. For it was " steamer night," — as that momentous day of reckoning before the sailing of the regular mail steamer was briefly known to commercial San Francisco, — and Mr. Nott was subject at such times to severely practical relapses. A swinging light seemed to bring into greater relief that peculiar encased casket-like security of the low-timbered, tightly-fitting apartment, with its toy-like utilities of space, and made the pretty oval face of Rosey Nott appear a characteristic ornament. The sliding door of the cabin communicated with the main deck, now roofed in and partitioned off so as to form a small passage that led to the open starboard gangway, where a narrow, inclosed staircase built on the ship's side took the place of the ship's ladder under her counter, and opened in the street.

A dash of rain against the window caused Rosey to lift her eyes from her book.

" It's much nicer here than at the ranch, father," she said coaxingly, " even leaving alone its being a beautiful ship instead of a shanty; the wind don't whistle through the cracks and blow out the candle when you're reading, nor the rain spoil your things hung up against the wall. And you look more like a gentleman sitting in his own — ship — you know, looking over his bills and getting ready to give his orders."

Vague and general as Miss Rosey's compliment was, it had its full effect upon her father, who was at times dimly conscious of his hopeless rusticity and its incongruity with his surroundings. " Yes," he said awkwardly, with a slight relaxation of his aggressive attitude; "yes, in course it's more bang-up style, but it don't pay — Rosey — it don't pay. Yer 's the Pontiac that oughter be bringin' in, ez rents go, at least three hundred a month, don't make her taxes. I bin thinkin' seriously of sellin' her."

As Rosey knew her father had experienced this serious contemplation on the first of every month for the last two years, and cheerfully ignored it the next day, she only said, " I 'm sure the vacant rooms and lofts are all rented, father."

" That 's it," returned Mr. Nott thoughtfully, plucking at his bushy whiskers with his fingers and thumb as if he were removing dead and sapless incumbrances in their growth, " that 's just what it is — them 's ez in it themselves don't pay, and them ez haz left their goods — the goods don't pay. The feller ez stored them iron sugar kettles in the forehold, after trying to get me to make another advance on 'em, sez he believes he 'll have to sacrifice 'em to me after all, and only begs I 'd give him a chance of buying back the half of 'em ten years from now, at double what I advanced him. The chap that left them five hundred cases of hair dye 'tween decks and then skipped out to Sacramento, met me the other day in the street and advised me to use a bottle ez an advertisement, or try it on the starn of the Pontiac for fire-proof paint. That foolishness ez all he's good for. And yet thar might be suthin' in the paint, if a feller had nigger luck. Ther's that New York chap ez bought up them damaged boxes of plug terbaker for fifty dollars a thousand, and sold 'em for foundations for that new building in Sansome Street at a thousand clear profit. It's all luck, Rosey."

The girl's eyes had wandered again to the pages of her book. Perhaps she was already familiar with the text of her father's monologue. But recognizing an additional querulousness in his voice, she laid the book aside and patiently folded her hands in her lap.

" That's right — for I 've suthin' to tell ye. The fact is Sleight wants to buy the Pontiac out and out just ez she stands with the two fifty vara lots she stands on."

" Sleight wants to buy her ? Sleight?" echoed Rosey incredulously.

" You bet! Sleight — the big financier, the smartest man in 'Frisco."

" What does he want to buy her for? " asked Rosey, knitting her pretty brows.

The apparently simple question suddenly puzzled Mr. Nott. He glanced feebly at his daughter's face, and frowned in vacant irritation. " That's so," he said, drawing a long breath; " there's suthin' in that."

" What did he *say?* " continued the young girl, impatiently.

" Not much. ' You've got the Pontiac, Nott,' sez he. ' You bet! ' sez I. ' What 'll you take for her and the lot she stands on? ' sez he, short and sharp. Some fellers, Rosey," said Nott, with a cunning smile, " would hev blurted out a big figger and been cotched. That ain't my style. I just looked at him. ' I 'll wait fur your figgers until next steamer day,' sez he, and off he goes like a shot. He 's awfully sharp, Rosey."

" But if he is sharp, father, and he really

wants to buy the ship," returned Rosey, thoughtfully, "it's only because he knows it's valuable property, and not because he likes it as we do. He can't take that value away even if we don't sell it to him, and all the while we have the comfort of the dear old Pontiac, don't you see?"

This exhaustive commercial reasoning was so sympathetic to Mr. Nott's instincts that he accepted it as conclusive. He, however, deemed it wise to still preserve his practical attitude. " But that don't make it pay by the month, Rosey. Suthin' must be done. I'm thinking I'll clean out that photographer."

"Not just after he's taken such a pretty view of the cabin front of the Pontiac from the street, father! No! He's going to give us a copy, and put the other in a shop window in Montgomery Street."

" That's so," said Mr. Nott, musingly; "it's no slouch of an advertisement. 'The Pontiac,' the property of A. Nott, Esq., of

St. Jo, Missouri. Send it on to your aunt
Phœbe ; sorter make the old folks open their
eyes — oh ? Well, seein' he 's been to some
expense fittin' up an entrance from the other
street, we 'll let him slide. But as to that
d——d old Frenchman Ferrers, in the next
loft, with his stuck-up airs and high falutin
style, we must get quit of him ; he 's regularly gouged me in that ere horsehair speki-
lation."

"How can you say that, father ! " said
Rosey, with a slight increase of color. " It
was your own offer. You know those bales
of curled horsehair were left behind by the
late tenant to pay his rent. When Mr. de
Ferrières rented the room afterwards, you
told him you 'ld throw them in in the place
of repairs and furniture. It was your own
offer."

" Yes, but I did n't reckon ther 'd ever be
a big price per pound paid for the darned
stuff for sofys and cushions and sich."

"How do you know *he* knew it, father ? "
responded Rosey.

"Then why did he look so silly at first, and then put on airs when I joked him about it, eh?"

"Perhaps he did n't understand your joking, father. He 's a foreigner, and shy and proud, and — not like the others. I don't think he knew what you meant then, any more than he believed he was making a bargain before. He may be poor, but I think he 's been — a — a — gentleman."

The young girl's animation penetrated even Mr. Nott's slow comprehension. Her novel opposition, and even the prettiness it enhanced, gave him a dull premonition of pain. His small round eyes became abstracted, his mouth remained partly open, even his fresh color slightly paled.

"You seem to have been takin' stock of this yer man, Rosey," he said, with a faint attempt at archness; "if he war n't ez old ez a crow, for all his young feathers, I 'd think he was makin' up to you."

But the passing glow had faded from her

young cheeks, and her eyes wandered again to her book. " He pays his rent regularly every steamer night," she said, quietly, as if dismissing an exhausted subject, " and he 'll be here in a moment, I dare say." She took up her book, and leaning her head on her hand, once more became absorbed in its pages.

An uneasy silence followed. The rain beat against the windows, the ticking of a clock became audible, but still Mr. Nott sat with vacant eyes fixed on his daughter's face, and the constrained smile on his lips. He was conscious that he had never seen her look so pretty before, yet he could not tell why this was no longer an unalloyed satisfaction. Not but that he had always accepted the admiration of others for her as a matter of course, but for the first time he became con-scious that she not only had an interest in others, but apparently a superior knowledge of them. How did she know these things about this man, and why had she only now

8

accidentally spoken of them ? *He* would have done so. All this passed so vaguely through his unreflective mind, that he was unable to retain any decided impression, but the far-reaching one that his lodger had obtained some occult influence over her through the exhibition of his baleful skill in the horse-hair speculation. " Them tricks is likely to take a young girl's fancy. I must look arter her," he said to himself softly.

A slow regular step in the gangway interrupted his paternal reflections. Hastily buttoning across his chest the pea-jacket which he usually wore at home as a single concession to his nautical surroundings, he drew himself up with something of the assumption of a ship-master, despite certain bucolic suggestions of his boots and legs. The footsteps approached nearer, and a tall figure suddenly stood in the doorway.

It was a figure so extraordinary that even in the strange masquerade of that early civilization it was remarkable; a figure with

whom father and daughter were already
familiar without abatement of wonder — the
figure of a rejuvenated old man, padded,
powdered, dyed, and painted to the verge of
caricature, but without a single suggestion
of ludicrousness or humor. A face so arti-
ficial that it seemed almost a mask, but, like
a mask, more pathetic than amusing. He
was dressed in the extreme of fashion of a
dozen years before ; his pearl gray trousers
strapped tightly over his varnished boots,
his voluminous satin cravat and high collar
embraced his rouged cheeks and dyed whiskers, his closely-buttoned frock coat clinging
to a waist that seemed accented by stays.

He advanced two steps into the cabin with
an upright precision of motion that might
have hid the infirmities of age, and said
deliberately with a foreign accent : —

" You-r-r ac-coumpt ? "

In the actual presence of the apparition
Mr. Nott's dignified resistance wavered. But
glancing uneasily at his daughter and seeing

her calm eyes fixed on the speaker without embarrassment, he folded his arms stiffly, and with a lofty simulation of examining the ceiling, said, —

" Ahem ! Rosa ! The gentleman's account."

It was an infelicitous action. For the stranger, who evidently had not noticed the presence of the young girl before, started, took a step quickly forward, bent stiffly but profoundly over the little hand that held the account, raised it to his lips, and with " a thousand pardons, mademoiselle," laid a small canvas bag containing the rent before the disorganized Mr. Nott and stiffly vanished.

That night was a troubled one to the simple-minded proprietor of the good ship Pontiac. Unable to voice his uneasiness by further discussion, but feeling that his late discomposing interview with his lodger demanded some marked protest, he absented himself on the plea of business during the rest of the evening, happily to his daughter's utter obliviousness of the reason. Lights were burning brilliantly in counting-rooms and offices, the feverish life of the mercantile city was at its height. With a vague idea of entering into immediate negotiations with Mr. Sleight for the sale of the ship — as a direct way out of his present perplexity, he bent his steps towards the financier's office, but paused and turned back before reaching the door. He made his way to the wharf and gazed abstractedly at the lights reflected in the dark, tremulous, jelly-like water. But wherever he went he was accompanied by the absurd figure of his lodger — a figure he had hitherto laughed at or half pitied, but which now, to his bewildered comprehension, seemed to have a fateful significance. Here a new idea seized him, and he hurried back to the ship, slackening his pace only when he arrived as his own doorway. Here he paused a moment and slowly ascended the staircase. When he reached the passage he coughed slightly and paused again. Then he pushed open the door of the darkened cabin and called softly : —

"Rosey!"

"What is it, father?" said Rosey's voice from the little state-room on the right — Rosey's own bower.

"Nothing!" said Mr. Nott, with an affectation of languid calmness; "I only wanted to know if you was comfortable. It's an awful busy night in town."

"Yes, father."

"I reckon thar's tons o' gold goin' to the States to-morrow."

"Yes, father."

"Pretty comfortable, eh?"

"Yes, father."

"Well, I'll browse round a spell, and turn in myself, soon."

"Yes, father."

Mr. Nott took down a hanging lantern, lit it, and passed out into the gangway. Another lamp hung from the companion hatch

to light the tenants to the lower deck, whence
he descended. This deck was divided fore
and aft by a partitioned passage, — the lofts
or apartments being lighted from the ports,
and one or two by a door cut through the
ship's side communicating with an alley on
either side. This was the case with the loft
occupied by Mr. Nott's strange lodger, which,
besides a door in the passage, had this independent communication with the alley. Nott
had never known him to make use of the
latter door; on the contrary, it was his regular habit to issue from his apartment at
three o'clock every afternoon, dressed as
he has been described, stride deliberately
through the passage to the upper deck and
thence into the street, where his strange figure was a feature of the principal promenade
for two or three hours, returning as regularly at eight o'clock to the ship and the
seclusion of his loft. Mr. Nott paused before the door, under the pretence of throwing the light before him into the shadows of

the forecastle; all was silent within. He was turning back when he was impressed by the regular recurrence of a peculiar rustling sound which he had at first referred to the rubbing of the wires of the swinging lantern against his clothing. He set down the light and listened; the sound was evidently on the other side of the partition; the sound of some prolonged, rustling, scraping movement, with regular intervals. Was it due to another of Mr. Nott's unprofitable tenants — the rats? No. A bright idea flashed upon Mr. Nott's troubled mind. It was de Ferrières snoring! He smiled grimly. "Wonder if Rosey'd call him a gentleman if she heard that," he chuckled to himself as he slowly made his way back to the cabin and the small state-room opposite to his daughter's. During the rest of the night he dreamed of being compelled to give Rosey in marriage to his strange lodger, who added insult to the outrage by snoring audibly through the marriage service.

Meantime, in her cradle-like nest in her nautical bower, Miss Rosey slumbered as lightly. Waking from a vivid dream of Venice — a child's Venice — seen from the swelling deck of the proudly-riding Pontiac, she was so impressed as to rise and cross on tiptoe to the little slanting port-hole. Morning was already dawning over the flat, straggling city, but from every counting-house and magazine the votive tapers of the feverish worshipers of trade and mammon were still flaring fiercely.

II.

The day following "steamer night" was usually stale and flat at San Francisco. The reaction from the feverish exaltation of the previous twenty-four hours was seen in the listless faces and lounging feet of promenaders, and was notable in the deserted offices and warehouses still redolent of last night's

gas, and strewn with the dead ashes of last
night's fires. There was a brief pause before the busy life which ran its course from
"steamer day" to steamer day was once
more taken up. In that interval a few anxious speculators and investors breathed
freely, some critical situation was relieved,
or some impending catastrophe momentarily
averted. In particular, a singular stroke of
good fortune that morning befell Mr. Nott.
He not only secured a new tenant, but, as
he sagaciously believed, introduced into the
Pontiac a counteracting influence to the subtle fascinations of de Ferrières.

The new tenant apparently possessed a
combination of business shrewdness and
brusque frankness that strongly impressed
his landlord. "You see, Rosey," said Nott,
complacently describing the interview to his
daughter, "when I sorter intimated in a
keerless kind o' way that sugar kettles and
hair dye was about played out ez securities,
he just planked down the money for two

months in advance. 'There,' sez he, 'that's *your* security — now where's *mine?*' 'I reckon I don't hitch on, pardner,' sez I; 'security what for?' ''Spose you sell the ship?' sez he, 'afore the two months is up. I've heard that old Sleight wants to buy her.' 'Then you gets back your money,' sez I. 'And lose my room,' sez he; 'not much, old man. You sign a paper that who-ever buys the ship inside o' two months hez to buy *me* ez a tenant with it; that's on the square.' So I sign the paper. It was mighty cute in the young feller, wasn't it?" he said, scanning his daughter's pretty puz-zled face a little anxiously; "and don't you see ez I ain't goin' to sell the Pontiac, it's just about ez cute in me, eh? He's a con-tractor somewhere around yer, and wants to be near his work. So he takes the room next to the Frenchman, that that ship captain quit for the mines, and succeeds naterally to his chest and things. He's mighty peart-looking, that young feller, Rosey — long black moustaches, all his own color, Rosey — and he's a regular high-stepper, you bet. I reckon he's not only been a gentleman, but ez *now*. Some o' them contractors are very high-toned!"

"I don't think we have any right to give him the captain's chest, father," said Rosey; "there may be some private things in it. There were some letters and photographs in the hair-dye man's trunk that you gave the photographer."

"That's just it, Rosey," returned Abner Nott with sublime unconsciousness, "photographs and love letters you can't sell for cash, and I don't mind givin' 'em away, if they kin make a feller creature happy."

"But, father, have we the *right* to give 'em away?"

"They're collateral security, Rosey," said her father grimly. "Co-la-te-ral," he continued, emphasizing each syllable by tapping the fist of one hand in the open palm of the other. "Co-la-te-ral is the word the big business sharps yer about call 'em. You can't get round that." He paused a moment, and then, as a new idea seemed to be painfully borne in his round eyes, continued cautiously: " Was that the reason why you would n't touch any of them dresses from the trunks of that opery gal ez skedaddled for Sacramento ? And yet them trunks I regularly bought at auction — Rosey — at auction, on spec — and they did n't realize the cost of drayage."

A slight color mounted to Rosey's face. " No," she said, hastily, " not that." Hesitating a moment she then drew softly to his side, and, placing her arms around his neck, turned his broad, foolish face towards her own. " Father," she began, " when mother died, would *you* have liked anybody to take her trunks and paw round her things and wear them ? "

" When your mother died, just this side o' Sweetwater, Rosey," said Mr. Nott, with beaming unconsciousness, " she had n't any trunks. I reckon she had n't even an extra gown hanging up in the wagin, 'cept the petticoat ez she had wrapped around yer. It was about ez much ez we could do to skirmish round with Injins, alkali, and cold, and we sorter forgot to dress for dinner. She never thought, Rosey, that you and me would live to be inhabitin' a paliss of a real ship. Ef she had she would have died a proud woman."

He turned his small, loving, boar-like eyes upon her as a preternaturally innocent and trusting companion of Ulysses might have regarded the transforming Circe. Rosey turned away with the faintest sigh. The habitual look of abstraction returned to her eyes as if she had once more taken refuge in her own ideal world. Unfortunately the change did not escape either the sensitive observation or the fatuous misconception of the sagacious parent. " Ye 'll be mountin' a few furbelows and fixins, Rosey, I reckon, ez only natural. Mebbee ye 'll have to prink

up a little now that we 've got a gentleman
contractor in the ship. I 'll see what I kin
pick up in Montgomery Street." And indeed he succeeded a few hours later in ac-
complishing with equal infelicity his gener-
ous design. When she returned from her
household tasks she found on her berth a
purple velvet bonnet of extraordinary make,
and a pair of white satin slippers. " They 'll
do for a start off, Rosey," he explained,
" and I got 'em at my figgers."

"But I go out so seldom, father, and a
bonnet " —

" That 's so," interrupted Mr. Nott, complacently, " it might be jest ez well for a
young gal like yer to appear ez if she *did*
go out, or would go out if she wanted to. So
you kin be wearin' that ar headstall kinder
like this evening when the contractor 's here,
ez if you 'd jest come in from a *pasear*."

Miss Rosey did not however immediately
avail herself of her father's purchase, but
contented herself with the usual scarlet rib-

bon that like a snood confined her brown hair, when she returned to her tasks. The space between the galley and the bulwarks had been her favorite resort in summer when not actually engaged in household work. It was now lightly roofed over with boards and tarpaulin against the winter rain, but still afforded her a veranda-like space before the galley door, where she could read or sew, looking over the bow of the Pontiac to the tossing bay or the further range of the Contra Costa hills.

Hither Miss Rosey brought the purple prodigy, partly to please her father, partly with a view of subjecting it to violent radical changes. But after trying it on before the tiny mirror in the galley once or twice, her thoughts wandered away, and she fell into one of her habitual reveries seated on a little stool before the galley door.

She was roused from it by the slight shaking and rattling of the doors of a small hatch on the deck, not a dozen yards from where she sat. It had been evidently fastened from below during the wet weather, but as she gazed, the fastenings were removed, the doors were suddenly lifted, and the head and shoulders of a young man emerged from the deck. Partly from her father's description, and partly from the impossibility of its being anybody else, she at once conceived it to be the new lodger. She had time to note that he was young and good-looking, graver perhaps than became his sudden pantomimic appearance, but before she could observe him closely, he had turned, closed the hatch with a certain familiar dexterity, and walked slowly towards the bows. Even in her slight bewilderment, she observed that his step upon the deck seemed different to her father's or the photographer's, and that he laid his hand on various objects with a half-caressing ease and habit. Presently he paused and turned back, and glancing at the galley door for the first time encountered her wondering eyes.

It seemed so evident that she had been a

9

curious spectator of his abrupt entrance on deck that he was at first disconcerted and confused. But after a second glance at her he appeared to resume his composure, and advanced a little defiantly towards the galley.

"I suppose I frightened you, popping up the fore hatch just now?"

"The what?" asked Rosey.

"The fore hatch," he repeated impatiently, indicating it with a gesture.

"And that's the fore hatch?" she said abstractedly. "You seem to know ships."

"Yes — a little," he said quietly. "I was below, and unfastened the hatch to come up the quickest way and take a look round. I've just hired a room here," he added explanatorily.

"I thought so," said Rosey simply; "you're the contractor?"

"The contractor! — oh, yes! You seem to know it all."

"Father's told me."

"Oh, he's your father — Nott? Certainly. I see now," he continued, looking at her with a half repressed smile. "Certainly, Miss Nott, good morning," he half added and walked towards the companion way. Something in the direction of his eyes as he turned away made Rosey lift her hands to her head. She had forgotten to remove her father's baleful gift.

She snatched it off and ran quickly to the companion way.

"Sir!" she called.

The young man turned half way down the steps and looked up. There was a faint color in her cheeks, and her pretty brown hair was slightly disheveled from the hasty removal of the bonnet.

"Father's very particular about strangers being on this deck," she said a little sharply.

"Oh — ah — I'm sorry I intruded."

"I — I — thought I'd tell you," said Rosey, frightened by her boldness into a feeble anti-climax.

" Thank you."

She came back slowly to the galley and
picked up the unfortunate bonnet with a
slight sense of remorse. Why should she
feel angry with her poor father's unhappy
offering? And what business had this
strange young man to use the ship so famil-
iarly? Yet she was vaguely conscious that
she and her father, with all their love and
their domestic experience of it, lacked a certain instinctive ease in its possession that
the half indifferent stranger had shown on
first treading its deck. She walked to the
hatchway and examined it with a new interest. Succeeding in lifting the hatch, she
gazed at the lower deck. As she already
knew the ladder had long since been removed
to make room for one of the partitions, the
only way the stranger could have reached it
was by leaping to one of the rings. To make
sure of this she let herself down holding on
to the rings, and dropped a couple of feet to
the deck below. She was in the narrow

passage her father had penetrated the previous night. Before her was the door leading to de Ferrières's loft, always locked. It was silent within; it was the hour when the old Frenchman made his habitual promenade in the city. But the light from the newly-opened hatch allowed her to see more of the mysterious recesses of the forward bulkhead than she had known before, and she was startled by observing another yawning hatchway at her feet from which the closely-fitting door had been lifted, and which the new lodger had evidently forgotten to close again. The young girl stooped down and peered cautiously into the black abyss. Nothing was to be seen, nothing heard but the distant gurgle and click of water in some remoter depth. She replaced the hatch and returned by way of the passage to the cabin.

When her father came home that night she briefly recounted the interview with the new lodger, and her discovery of his curiosity. She did this with a possible increase of her usual shyness and abstraction, and apparently more as a duty than a colloquial recreation. But it pleased Mr. Nott also to give it more than his usual misconception. " Looking round the ship, was he — eh, Rosey?" he said with infinite archness. " In course, kinder sweepin' round the galley, and offerin' to fetch you wood and water, eh?" Even when the young girl had picked up her book with the usual faint smile of affectionate tolerance, and then drifted away in its pages, Mr. Nott chuckled audibly. " I reckon old Frenchy did n't come by when the young one was bedevlin' you there."

" What, father?" said Rosy, lifting her abstracted eyes to his face.

At the moment it seemed impossible that any human intelligence could have suspected deceit or duplicity in Rosey's clear gaze. But Mr. Nott's intelligence was superhuman. "I was sayin' that Mr. Ferrières did n't happen in while the young feller was there — eh?"

"No, father," answered Rosey, with an effort to follow him out of the pages of her book. "Why?"

But Mr. Nott did not reply. Later in the evening he awkwardly waylaid the new lodger before the cabin door as that gentleman would have passed on to his room.

"I'm afraid," said the young man, glancing at Rosey, "that I intruded upon your daughter to-day. I was a little curious to see the old ship, and I did n't know what part of it was private."

"There ain't no private part to this yer ship — that ez, 'cepting the rooms and lofts," said Mr. Nott, authoritatively. Then, subjecting the anxious look of his daughter to his usual faculty for misconception, he added, "Thar ain't no place whar you have n't as much right to go ez any other man; thar ain't any man, furriner or Amerykan, young or old, dyed or undyed, ez hev got any better rights. You hear me, young fellow. Mr. Renshaw — my darter. My darter — Mr.

Renshaw. Rosey, give the gentleman a chair. She's only jest come in from a promeynade, and hez jest taken off her bonnet," he added, with an arch look at Rosey, and a hurried look around the cabin, as if he hoped to see the missing gift visible to the general eye. " So take a seat a minit, won't ye?"

But Mr. Renshaw, after an observant glance at the young girl's abstracted face, brusquely excused himself. "I've got a letter to write," he said, with a half bow to Rosey. "Good night."

He crossed the passage to the room that had been assigned to him, and closing the door gave way to some irritability of temper in his efforts to light the lamp and adjust his writing materials. For his excuse to Mr. Nott was more truthful than most polite pretexts. He had, indeed, a letter to write, and one that, being yet young in duplicity, the near presence of his host rendered difficult. For it ran as follows : —

" DEAR SLEIGHT,

" As I found I could n't get a chance to make any examination of the ship except as occasion offered, I just went in to rent lodgings in her from the God-forsaken old ass who owns her, and here I am a tenant for two months. I contracted for that time in case the old fool should sell out to some one else before. Except that she 's cut up a little between decks by the partitions for lofts that that Pike County idiot has put into her, she looks but little changed, and her *forehold*, as far as I can judge, is intact. It seems that Nott bought her just as she stands, with her cargo half out, but he was n't here when she broke cargo. If anybody else had bought her but this cursed Missourian, who has n't got the hayseed out of his hair, I might have found out something from him, and saved myself this kind of fooling, which is n't in my line. If I could get possession of a loft on the main deck, well forward, just over the fore-hold, I could satisfy myself in a few hours, but the loft is rented by that crazy Frenchman who parades Montgomery Street every afternoon, and though old Pike County wants to turn him out, I 'm afraid I can't get it for a week to come.

"If anything should happen to me, just you waltz down here and corral my things at once, for this old frontier pirate has a way of confiscating his lodgers' trunks.

"Yours, DICK."

III.

If Mr. Renshaw indulged in any further curiosity regarding the interior of the Pontiac, he did not make his active researches manifest to Rosey. Nor, in spite of her father's invitation, did he again approach the galley — a fact which gave her her first vague impression in his favor. He seemed also to avoid the various advances which Mr. Nott appeared impelled to make, when-

ever they met in the passage, but did so
without seemingly avoiding *her*, and marked
his half contemptuous indifference to the
elder Nott by an increase of respect to the
young girl. She would have liked to ask
him something about ships, and was sure
his conversation would have been more in-
teresting than that of old Captain Bower,
to whose cabin he had succeeded, who had
once told her a ship was the " devil's hen-
coop." She would have liked also to explain to him that she was not in the habit of
wearing a purple bonnet. But her thoughts
were presently engrossed by an experience
which interrupted the even tenor of her
young life.

She had been, as she afterwards remembered, impressed with a nervous restlessness
one afternoon, which made it impossible for
her to perform her ordinary household duties,
or even to indulge her favorite recreation
of reading or castle building. She wandered
over the ship, and, impelled by the same

vague feeling of unrest, descended to the lower deck and the forward bulkhead where she had discovered the open hatch. It had not been again disturbed, nor was there any trace of further exploration. A little ashamed, she knew not why, of revisiting the scene of Mr. Renshaw's researches, she was turning back when she noticed that the door which communicated with de Ferrières's loft was partly open. The circumstance was so unusual that she stopped before it in surprise. There was no sound from within; it was the hour when its queer occupant was always absent; he must have forgotten to lock the door or it had been unfastened by other hands. After a moment of hesitation she pushed it further open and stepped into the room.

By the dim light of two port-holes she could see that the floor was strewn and piled with the contents of a broken bale of curled horse hair, of which a few untouched bales still remained against the wall. A heap of

morocco skins, some already cut in the form
of chair cushion covers, and a few cushions
unfinished and unstuffed lay in the light of
the ports, and gave the apartment the appearance of a cheap workshop. A rude instrument for combing the horse hair, awls,
buttons, and thread heaped on a small bench
showed that active work had been but re-
cently interrupted. A cheap earthenware
ewer and basin on the floor, and a pallet
made of an open bale of horse hair, on which
a ragged quilt and blanket were flung, in-
dicated that the solitary worker dwelt and
slept beside his work.

The truth flashed upon the young girl's
active brain, quickened by seclusion and fed
by solitary books. She read with keen eyes
the miserable secret of her father's strange
guest in the poverty-stricken walls, in the
mute evidences of menial handicraft per-
formed in loneliness and privation, in this
piteous adaptation of an accident to save the
conscious shame of premeditated toil. She

knew now why he had stammeringly refused to receive her father's offer to buy back the goods he had given him ; she knew now how hardly gained was the pittance that paid his rent and supported his childish vanity and grotesque pride. From a peg in the corner hung the familiar masquerade that hid his poverty — the pearl-gray trousers, the black frock coat, the tall shining hat — in hideous contrast to the penury of his surroundings. But if *they* were here, where was *he*, and in what new, disguise had he escaped from his poverty ? A vague uneasiness caused her to hesitate and return to the open door. She had nearly reached it when her eye fell on the pallet which it partly illuminated. A singular resemblance in the ragged heap made her draw closer. The faded quilt was a dressing-gown, and clutching its folds lay a white, wasted hand.

The emigrant childhood of Rose Nott had been more than once shadowed by scalping knives, and she was acquainted with Death.

She went fearlessly to the couch, and found
that the dressing-gown was only an en-
wrapping of the emaciated and lifeless body
of de Ferrières. She did not retreat or call
for help, but examined him closely. He was
unconscious, but not pulseless ; he had evidently been strong enough to open the door
for air or succor, but had afterward fallen in
a fit on the couch. She flew to her father's
locker and the galley fire, returned, and shut
the door behind her, and by the skillful use
of hot water and whiskey soon had the satisfaction of seeing a faint color take the place
of the faded rouge in the ghastly cheeks.
She was still chafing his hands when he
slowly opened his eyes. With a start, he
made a quick attempt to push aside her
hands and rise. But she gently restrained
him.

"Eh — what!" he stammered, throwing
his face back from hers with an effort and
trying to turn it to the wall.

"You have been ill," she said quietly.
"Drink this."

With his face still turned away he lifted the cup to his chattering teeth. When he had drained it he threw a trembling glance around the room and at the door.

"There's no one been here but myself," she said quickly. "I happened to see the door open as I passed. I did n't think it worth while to call any one."

The searching look he gave her turned into an expression of relief, which, to her infinite uneasiness, again feebly lightened into one of antiquated gallantry. He drew the dressing-gown around him with an air.

"Ah! it is a goddess, Mademoiselle, that has deigned to enter the cell where — where — I — amuse myself. It is droll — is it not? I came here to make — what you call — the experiment of your father's fabric. I make myself — ha! ha! — like a workman. Ah, bah! the heat, the darkness, the plebeian motion make my head to go round. I stagger, I faint, I cry out, I fall. But what of that? The great God hears my cry and sends me an angel. *Voilà!*"

He attempted an easy gesture of gallantry, but overbalanced himself and fell sideways on the pallet with a gasp. Yet there was so much genuine feeling mixed with his grotesque affectation, so much piteous consciousness of the ineffectiveness of his falsehood, that the young girl, who had turned away, came back and laid her hand upon his arm.

"You must lie still and try to sleep," she said gently. "I will return again. Perhaps," she added, "there is some one I can send for?"

He shook his head violently. Then in his old manner added, "After Mádemoiselle — no one."

"I mean" — she hesitated; "have you no friends?"

"Friends, — ah! without doubt." He shrugged his shoulders. "But Mademoiselle will comprehend" —

"You are better now," said Rosey quickly, "and no one need know anything if you don't wish it. Try to sleep. You need not

10

lock the door when I go; I will see that no
one comes in."

He flushed faintly and averted his eyes.
" It is too droll, Mademoiselle, is it not ? "

" Of course it is," said Rosey, glancing
round the miserable room.

" And Mademoiselle is an angel."

He carried her hand to his lips humbly
— his first purely unaffected action. She
slipped through the door, and softly closed
it behind her.

Reaching the upper deck she was relieved
to find her father had not returned, and her
absence had been unnoticed. For she had
resolved to keep de Ferrières's secret to herself from the moment that she had unwittingly discovered it, and to do this and still
be able to watch over him without her
father's knowledge required some caution.
She was conscious of his strange aversion to
the unfortunate man without understanding the reason, but as she was in the habit
of entertaining his caprices more from af-

fectionate tolerance of his weakness than reverence of his judgment, she saw no disloyalty to him in withholding a confidence that might be disloyal to another. " It won't do father any good to know it," she said to herself, " and if it *did* it ought n't to," she added with triumphant feminine logic. But the impression made upon her by the spectacle she had just witnessed was stronger than any other consideration. The revelation of de Ferrières's secret poverty seemed a chapter from a romance of her own weaving; for a moment it lifted the miserable hero out of the depths of his folly and selfishness. She forgot the weakness of the man in the strength of his dramatic surroundings. It partly satisfied a craving she had felt; it was not exactly the story of the ship, as she had dreamed it, but it was an episode in her experience of it that broke its monotony. That she should soon learn, perhaps from de Ferrières's own lips, the true reason of his strange seclusion, and that it involved more than appeared to her now, she never for a moment doubted.

At the end of an hour she again knocked softly at the door, carrying some light nourishment she had prepared for him. He was asleep, but she was astounded to find that in the interval he had managed to dress himself completely in his antiquated finery. It was a momentary shock to the illusion she had been fostering, but she forgot it in the pitiable contrast between his haggard face and his pomatumed hair and beard, the jauntiness of his attire, and the collapse of his invalid figure. When she had satisfied herself that his sleep was natural, she busied herself softly in arranging the miserable apartment. With a few feminine touches she removed the slovenliness of misery, and placed the loose material and ostentatious evidences of his work on one side. Finding that he still slept, and knowing the importance of this natural medication, she placed the refreshment she had brought by his side and noiselessly quitted the apartment. Hurrying through the gathering darkness between decks, she once or twice thought she had heard footsteps, and paused, but encountering no one, attributed the impression to her over-consciousness. Yet she thought it prudent to go to the galley first, where she lingered a few moments before returning to the cabin. On entering she was a little startled at observing a figure seated at her father's desk, but was relieved at finding it was Mr. Renshaw.

He rose and put aside the book he had idly picked up. " I am afraid I am an intentional intruder this time, Miss Nott. But I found no one here, and I was tempted to look into this ship - shape little snuggery. You see the temptation got the better of me."

His voice and smile were so frank and pleasant, so free from his previous restraint, yet still respectful, so youthful yet manly, that Rosey was affected by them even in her preoccupation. Her eyes brightened and then dropped before his admiring glance. Had she known that the excitement of the last few hours had brought a wonderful charm into her pretty face, had aroused the slumbering life of her half-wakened beauty, she would have been more confused. As it was, she was only glad that the young man should turn out to be "nice." Perhaps he might tell her something about ships; perhaps if she had only known him longer she might, with de Ferrières's permission, have shared her confidence with him, and enlisted his sympathy and assistance. She contented herself with showing this anticipatory gratitude in her face as she begged him, with the timidity of a maiden hostess, to resume his seat.

But Mr. Renshaw seemed to talk only to make her talk, and I am forced to admit that Rosey found this almost as pleasant. It was not long before he was in possession of her simple history from the day of her

baby emigration to California to the trans-
fer of her childish life to the old ship, and
even of much of the romantic fancies she
had woven into her existence there. Whatever ulterior purpose he had in view, he listened as attentively as if her artless chronicle
was filled with practical information. Once,
when she had paused for breath, he said
gravely, " I must ask you to show me over
this wonderful ship some day that I may see
it with your eyes."

" But I think you know it already better
than I do," said Rosey with a smile.

Mr. Renshaw's brow clouded slightly.
" Ah," he said, with a touch of his former
restraint ; " and why ? "

" Well," said Rosey timidly, " I thought
you went round and touched things in a
familiar way as if you had handled them
before."

The young man raised his eyes to Rosey's
and kept them there long enough to bring
back his gentler expression. " Then, because

I found you trying on a very queer bonnet the first day I saw you," he said, mischievously, " I ought to believe you were in the habit of wearing one."

In the first flush of mutual admiration young people are apt to find a laugh quite as significant as a sigh for an expression of sympathetic communion, and this masterstroke of wit convulsed them both. In the midst of it Mr. Nott entered the cabin. But the complacency with which he viewed the evident perfect understanding of the pair was destined to suffer some abatement. Rosey, suddenly conscious that she was in some way participating in ridicule of her father through his unhappy gift, became embarrassed. Mr. Renshaw's restraint returned with the presence of the old man. In vain, at first, Abner Nott strove with profound levity to indicate his arch comprehension of the situation, and in vain, later, becoming alarmed, he endeavored, with cheerful gravity, to indicate his utter obliv-

iousness of any but a business significance
in their *tête-à-tête*.

"I ought n't to hev intruded, Rosey," he
said, "when you and the gentleman were
talkin' of contracts, mebbee; but don't mind
me. I'm on the fly, anyhow, Rosey dear,
hevin' to see a man round the corner."

But even the attitude of withdrawing did
not prevent the exit of Renshaw to his
apartment and of Rosey to the galley. Left
alone in the cabin, Abner Nott felt in the
knots and tangles of his beard for a reason.
Glancing down at his prodigious boots which,
covered with mud and gravel, strongly em-
phasized his agricultural origin, and gave
him a general appearance of standing on his
own broad acres, he was struck with an idea.
"It's them boots," he whispered to himself,
softly; "they somehow don't seem 'xactly to
trump or follow suit in this yer cabin; they
don't hitch into anythin', but jist slosh
round loose, and so to speak play it alone.
And them young critters nat'rally feels it and

gets out o' the way." Acting upon this instinct with his usual precipitate caution, he
at once proceeded to the nearest second-hand
shop, and, purchasing a pair of enormous
carpet slippers, originally the property of a
gouty sea-captain, reappeared with a strong
suggestion of newly upholstering the cabin.
The improvement, however, was fraught with
a portentous circumstance. Mr. Nott's footsteps, which usually announced his approach
all over the ship, became stealthy and in-
audible.

Meantime Miss Rosey had taken advantage
of the absence of her father to visit her
patient. To avoid attracting attention she
did not take a light, but groped her way to
the lower deck and rapped softly at the door.
It was instantly opened by de Ferrières.
He had apparently appreciated the few
changes she had already made in the room,
and had himself cleared away the pallet
from which he had risen to make two low
seats against the wall. Two bits of candle

placed on the floor illuminated the beams above, the dressing - gown was artistically draped over the solitary chair, and a pile of cushions formed another seat. With elaborate courtesy he handed Miss Rosey to the chair. He looked pale and weak, though the gravity of the attack had evidently passed. Yet he persisted in remaining standing. "If I sit," he explained with a gesture, " I shall again disgrace myself by sleeping in Mademoiselle's presence. Yes! I shall sleep — I shall dream — and wake to find her gone ? "

More embarrassed by his recovery than when he was lying helplessly before her, she said hesitatingly that she was glad he was better, and that she hoped he liked the broth.

" It was manna from heaven, Mademoiselle. See, I have taken it all — every precious drop. What else could I have done for Mademoiselle's kindness ? "

He showed her the empty bowl. A swift conviction came upon her that the man had

been suffering from want of food. The
thought restored her self-possession even
while it brought the tears to her eyes. "I
wish you would let me speak to father — or
some one," she said impulsively, and stopped.

A quick and half insane gleam of terror
and suspicion lit up his deep eyes. "For
what, Mademoiselle! For an accident — that
is nothing — absolutely nothing, for I am
strong and well now — see!" he said tremblingly. "Or for a whim — for a folly you
may say, that they will misunderstand. No,
Mademoiselle is good, is wise. She will say
to herself, 'I understand, my friend Monsieur de Ferrières for the moment has a
secret. He would seem poor, he would take
the *rôle* of artisan, he would shut himself up
in these walls — perhaps I may guess why,
but it is his secret. I think of it no more.'"
He caught her hand in his with a gesture
that he would have made one of gallantry,
but that in its tremulous intensity became a
piteous supplication.

"I have said nothing, and will say nothing, if you wish it," said Rosey hastily; "but others may find out how you live here. This is not fit work for you. You seem to be a — a gentleman. You ought to be a lawyer, or a doctor, or in a bank," she continued timidly, with a vague enumeration of the prevailing degrees of local gentility.

He dropped her hand. "Ah! does not Mademoiselle comprehend that it is *because* I am a gentleman that there is nothing between it and this? Look!" he continued almost fiercely. "What if I told you it is the lawyer, it is the doctor, it is the banker that brings me, a gentleman, to this, eh? Ah, bah! What do I say? This is honest, what I do! But the lawyer, the banker, the doctor, what are they?" He shrugged his shoulders, and pacing the apartment with a furtive glance at the half anxious, half frightened girl, suddenly stopped, dragged a small portmanteau from behind the heap of bales and opened it. "Look, Mademoiselle,"

he said, tremulously lifting a handful of
worn and soiled letters and papers. "Look
— these are the tools of your banker, your
lawyer, your doctor. With this the banker
will make you poor, the lawyer will prove
you a thief, the doctor will swear you are
crazy, eh? What shall you call the work of
a gentleman — this " — he dragged the pile
of cushions forward — " or this ? "

To the young girl's observant eyes some
of the papers appeared to be of a legal or
official character, and others like bills of
lading, with which she was familiar. Their
half-theatrical exhibition reminded her of
some play she had seen ; they might be the
clue to some story, or the mere worthless
hoardings of a diseased fancy. Whatever
they were, de Ferrières did not apparently
care to explain further; indeed, the next
moment his manner changed to his old
absurd extravagance. " But this is stupid
for Mademoiselle to hear. What shall we
speak of ? Ah ! what *should* we speak of
in Mademoiselle's presence ? "

"But are not these papers valuable?" asked Rosey, partly to draw her host's thoughts back to their former channel.

"Perhaps." He paused and regarded the young girl fixedly. "Does Mademoiselle think so?"

"I don't know," said Rosey. "How should I?"

"Ah! if Mademoiselle thought so — if Mademoiselle would deign" — He stopped again and placed his hand upon his forehead. "It might be so!" he muttered.

"I must go now," said Rosey hurriedly, rising with an awkward sense of constraint. "Father will wonder where I am."

"I shall explain. I will accompany you Mademoiselle."

"No, no," said Rosey, quickly; "he must not know I have been here!" She stopped. The honest blush flew to her cheek, and then returned again, because she had blushed.

De Ferrières gazed at her with an exalted look. Then drawing himself to his full height, he said, with an exaggerated and indescribable gesture, "Go, my child, go. Tell your father that you have been alone and unprotected in the abode of poverty and suffering, but — that it was in the presence of Armand de Ferrières."

He threw open the door with a bow that nearly swept the ground, but did not again offer to take her hand. At once impressed and embarrassed at this crowning incongruity, her pretty lip trembled between a smile and a cry as she said, "Good-night," and slipped away into the darkness.

Erect and grotesque de Ferrières retained the same attitude until the sound of her footsteps was lost, when he slowly began to close the door. But a strong arm arrested it from without, and a large carpeted foot appeared at the bottom of the narrowing opening. The door yielded, and Mr. Abner Nott entered the room.

IV.

With an exclamation and a hurried glance around him, de Ferrières threw himself before the intruder. But slowly lifting his large hand, and placing it on his lodger's breast, he quietly overbore the sick man's feeble resistance with an impact of power that seemed almost as moral as it was physical. He did not appear to take any notice of the room or its miserable surroundings; indeed, scarcely of the occupant. Still pushing him, with abstracted eyes and immobile face, to the chair that Rosey had just quitted, he made him sit down, and then took up his own position on the pile of cushions opposite. His usually underdone complexion was of watery blueness; but his dull, abstracted glance appeared to exercise a certain dumb, narcotic fascination on his lodger.

11

"I mout," said Nott, slowly, " hev laid ye
out here on sight, without enny warnin',
or dropped ye in yer tracks in Montgomery
Street, wherever ther was room to work a
six-shooter in comf'ably ? Johnson, of Peta-
luny — him, ye know, ez had a game eye —
fetched Flynn comin' outer meetin' one
Sunday, and it was only on account of his
wife, and she a second-hand one, so to speak.
There was Walker, of Contra Costa, plugged
that young Sacramento chap, whose name
I disremember, full o' holes just ez *he* was
sayin' ' Good by' to his darter. I mout hev
done all this if it had settled things to
please me. For while you and Flynn and
that Sacramento chap ez all about the same
sort o' men, Rosey's a different kind from
their sort o' women."

"Mademoiselle is an angel ! " said de Ferrières, suddenly rising, with an excess of extravagance. "A saint ! Look ! I cram the
lie, ha ! down his throat who challenges it."

"Ef by mam'selle ye mean my Rosey,"

said Nott, quietly laying his powerful hands on de Ferrières's shoulders, and slowly pinning him down again upon his chair, " ye 're about right, though she ain't mam'selle yet. Ez I was sayin', I might hev killed you off hand if I hed thought it would hev been a good thing for Rosey."

"For her? Ah, well! Look, I am ready." interrupted de Ferrières, again springing to his feet, and throwing open his coat with both hands. " See! here at my heart — fire! "

" Ez I was sayin'," continued Nott, once more pressing the excited man down in his chair, " I might hev wiped ye out — and mebbee ye would n't hev keered — or *you* might hev wiped *me* out, and I mout hev said, ' Thank 'ee,' but I reckon this ain't a case for what 's comf'able for you and me. It 's what 's good for *Rosey*. And the thing to kalkilate is, what 's to be done."

His small round eyes for the first time rested on de Ferrières's face, and were quickly withdrawn. It was evident that this abstracted look, which had fascinated his lodger, was merely a resolute avoidance of de Ferrières's glance, and it became apparent later that this avoidance was due to a ludicrous appreciation of de Ferrières's attractions.

"And after we 've done *that* we must kalkilate what Rosey *is*, and what Rosey wants. P'raps, ye allow, *you* know what Rosey is? P'raps you 've seen her prance round in velvet bonnets and white satin slippers, and sich. P'raps you 've seen her readin' tracks and v'yages, without waitin' to spell a word, or catch her breath. But that ain't the Rosey ez *I* know. It 's a little child ez uster crawl in and out the tail-board of a Mizzouri wagon on the alcali pizoned plains, where there was n't another bit of God's mercy on yearth to be seen for miles and miles. It 's a little gal as uster hunger and thirst ez quiet and mannerly ez she now eats and drinks in plenty; whose voice was ez steady with Injins yelling round her nest in the leaves on Sweetwater ez in her purty cabin up yonder. *That's* the gal ez I know! That's the Rosey ez my ole woman puts into my arms one night arter we left Laramie when the fever was high, and sez, 'Abner,' sez she, 'the chariot is swingin' low for me to-night, but thar ain't room in it for her or you to git in or hitch on. Take her and rare her, so we kin all jine on the other shore,' sez she. And I'd knowed the other shore was n't no Kaliforny. And that night, p'raps, the chariot swung lower than ever before, and my ole woman stepped into it, and left me and Rosey to creep on in the old wagon alone. It's them kind o' things," added Mr. Nott thoughtfully, "that seem to pint to my killin' you on sight ez the best thing to be done. And yet Rosey might n't like it."

He had slipped one of his feet out of his huge carpet slippers, and, as he reached down to put it on again, he added calmly:

"And ez to yer marrying *her* it ain't to be done."

The utterly bewildered expression which transfigured de Ferrières's face at this announcement was unobserved by Nott's averted eyes, nor did he perceive that his listener the next moment straightened his erect figure and adjusted his cravat.

"Ef Rosey," he continued, "hez read in vy'ges and tracks in Eyetalian and French countries of such chaps ez you and kalkilates you 're the right kind to tie to, mebbee it mout hev done if you 'd been livin' over thar in a pallis, but somehow it don't jibe in over here and agree with a ship — and that ship lying comf'able ashore in San Francisco. You don't seem to suit the climate, you see, and your general gait is likely to stampede the other cattle. Agin," said Nott, with an ostentation of looking at his companion but really gazing on vacancy, "this fixed up, antique style of yours goes better with them ivy kivered ruins in Rome and

Palmyry that Rosey's mixed you up with, than it would yere. I ain't saying," he added as de Ferrières was about to speak, "I ain't sayin' ez that child ain't smitten with ye. It ain't no use to lie and say she don't prefer you to her old father, or young chaps of her own age and kind. I've seed it afor now. I suspicioned it afor I seed her slip out o' this place to-night. Thar! keep your hair on, such ez it is!" he added as de Ferrières attempted a quick deprecatory gesture. "I ain't askin yer how often she comes here, nor what she sez to you nor you to her. I ain't asked her and I don't ask you. I'll allow ez you've settled all the preliminaries and bought her the ring and sich; I'm only askin' you now, kalkilatin' you've got all the keerds in your own hand, what you'll take to step out and leave the board?"

The dazed look of de Ferrières might have forced itself even upon Nott's one-idead fatuity, had it not been a part of that gentleman's system delicately to look an-

other way at that moment so as not to em-
barrass his adversary's calculation. " Pardon," stammered de Ferrières, " but I do
not comprehend ! " He raised his hand to
his head. " I am not well — I am stupid.
Ah, mon Dieu ! "

" I ain't sayin'," added Nott more gently,
" ez you don't feel bad. It 's nat'ral. But
it ain't business. I 'm asking you," he continued, talking from his breast-pocket a large
wallet, " how much you 'll take in cash now,
and the rest next steamer day, to give up
Rosey and leave the ship."

De Ferrières staggered to his feet despite
Nott's restraining hand. " To leave Mademoiselle and leave the ship ? " he said hus-
kily, " is it not ? "

" In course. Yer can leave things yer
just ez you found 'em when you came, you
know," continued Nott, for the first time
looking around the miserable apartment.
" It 's a business job. I 'll take the bales
back ag'in, and you kin reckon up what
you 're out, countin' Rosey and loss o' time."

" He wishes me to go — he has said," repeated de Ferrières to himself thickly.

" Ef you mean *me* when you say *him*, and ez thar ain't any other man around, I reckon you do — ' yes ! ' "

" And he asks me — he — this man of the feet and the daughter — asks me — de Ferrières — what I will take," continued de Ferrières, buttoning his coat. " No ! it is a dream ! " He walked stiffly to the corner where his portmanteau lay, lifted it, and going to the outer door, a cut through the ship's side that communicated with the alley, unlocked it and flung it open to the night. A thick mist like the breath of the ocean flowed into the room.

" You ask me what I shall take to go," he said as he stood on the threshold. " I shall take what *you* cannot give, Monsieur, but what I would not keep if I stood here another moment. I take my Honor, Monsieur, and — I take my leave ! "

For a moment his grotesque figure was

outlined in the opening, and then disappeared as if he had dropped into an invisible ocean below. Stupefied and disconcerted at this complete success of his overtures, Abner Nott remained speechless, gazing at the vacant space until a cold influx of the mist recalled him. Then he rose and shuffled quickly to the door.

"Hi! Ferrers! Look yer — Say! Wot's your hurry, pardner?"

But there was no response. The thick mist, which hid the surrounding objects, seemed to deaden all sound also. After a moment's pause he closed the door, but did not lock it, and retreating to the centre of the room remained blinking at the two candles and plucking some perplexing problem from his beard. Suddenly an idea seized him. Rosey! Where was she? Perhaps it had been a preconcerted plan, and she had fled with him. Putting out the lights he stumbled hurriedly through the passage to the gangway above. The cabin-door was open ; there was the sound of voices — Renshaw's and Rosey's. Mr. Nott felt relieved but not unembarrassed. He would have avoided his daughter's presence that evening. But even while making this resolution with characteristic infelicity he blundered into the room. Rosey looked up with a slight start ; Renshaw's animated face was changed to its former expression of inward discontent.

"You came in so like a ghost, father," said Rosey with a slight peevishness that was new to her. "And I thought you were in town. Don't go, Mr. Renshaw."

But Mr. Renshaw intimated that he had already trespassed upon Miss Nott's time, and that no doubt her father wanted to talk with her. To his surprise and annoyance, however, Mr. Nott insisted on accompanying him to his room, and without heeding Renshaw's cold "Good-night," entered and closed the door behind him.

"P'rap's," said Mr. Nott with a troubled

air, "you disremember that when you first
kem here you asked me if you could hev
that 'er loft that the Frenchman had down
stairs."

"No, I don't remember it," said Renshaw
almost rudely. "But," he added, after a
pause, with the air of a man obliged to re-
vive a stale and unpleasant memory, "if I
did — what about it?"

"Nuthin', only that you kin hev it to-
morrow, ez that 'ere Frenchman is movin'
out," responded Nott. "I thought you was
sorter keen about it when you first kem."

"Umph! we 'll talk about it to-morrow."
Something in the look of wearied perplexity
with which Mr. Nott was beginning to regard his own *mal à propos* presence, arrested the young man's attention. "What's
the reason you did n't sell this old ship long
ago, take a decent house in the town, and
bring up your daughter like a lady?" he
asked with a sudden blunt good humor. But
even this implied blasphemy against the

habitation he worshiped did not prevent Mr. Nott from his usual misconstruction of the question.

"I reckon, now, Rosey's got high-flown ideas of livin' in a castle with ruins, eh?" he said cunningly.

"Have n't heard her say," returned Renshaw abruptly. "Good-night."

Firmly convinced that Rosey had been unable to conceal from Mr. Renshaw the influence of her dreams of a castellated future with de Ferrières, he regained the cabin. Satisfying himself that his daughter had retired, he sought his own couch. But not to sleep. The figure of de Ferrières, standing in the ship side and melting into the outer darkness, haunted him, and compelled him in dreams to rise and follow him through the alleys and by-ways of the crowded city. Again, it was a part of his morbid suspicion that he now invested the absent man with a potential significance and an unknown power. What deep-laid plans might he not form to possess himself of Rosey, of which he, Abner Nott, would be ignorant? Unchecked by the restraint of a father's roof he would now give full license to his power. "Said he'd take his Honor with him," muttered Abner to himself in the dim watches of the night; "lookin' at that sayin' in its right light, it looks bad."

V.

The elaborately untruthful account which Mr. Nott gave his daughter of de Ferrières's sudden departure was more fortunate than his usual equivocations. While it disappointed and slightly mortified her, it did not seem to her inconsistent with what she already knew of him. "Said his doctor had ordered him to quit town under an hour, owing to a comin' attack of hay fever, and he had a friend from furrin parts waitin' him at the Springs, Rosey," explained Nott, hesitating between his desire to avoid his daughter's eyes and his wish to observe her countenance.

"Was he worse? — I mean did he look badly, father?" inquired Rosey thoughtfully.

"I reckon not exackly bad. Kinder looked ez if he mout be worse soon ef he did n't hump hisself."

"Did you see him? — in his room?" asked Rosey anxiously. Upon the answer to this simple question depended the future confidential relations of father and daughter. If her father had himself detected the means by which his lodger existed, she felt that her own obligations to secrecy had been removed. But Mr. Nott's answer disposed of this vain hope. It was a response after his usual fashion to the question he *imagined* she artfully wished to ask, *i. e.* if he had discovered their rendezvous of the previous night. This it was part of his peculiar delicacy to ignore. Yet his reply showed that he had been unconscious of the one miserable secret that he might have read easily.

"I was there an hour or so — him and me alone — discussin' trade. I reckon he's got a good thing outer that curled horse hair, for I see he's got in an invoice o' cushions. I've stored 'em all in the forrard bulkhead until he sends for 'em, ez Mr. Renshaw hez taken the loft."

But although Mr. Renshaw had taken the loft, he did not seem in haste to occupy it. He spent part of the morning in uneasily pacing his room, in occasional sallies into the street from which he purposelessly returned, and once or twice in distant and furtive contemplation of Rosey at work in the galley. This last observation was not unnoticed by the astute Nott, who at once conceiving that he was nourishing a secret and hopeless passion for Rosey, began to consider whether it was not his duty to warn the young man of her preoccupied affections. But Mr. Renshaw's final disappearance obliged him to withhold his confidence till morning.

This time Mr. Renshaw left the ship with the evident determination of some settled purpose. He walked rapidly until he reached the counting-house of Mr. Sleight, when he was at once shown into a private office. In a few moments Mr. Sleight, a brusque but passionless man, joined him.

"Well," said Sleight, closing the door carefully. "What news?"

"None," said Renshaw bluntly. "Look here, Sleight," he added, turning to him suddenly. "Let me out of this game. I don't like it."

"Does that mean you've found nothing?" asked Sleight, sarcastically.

"It means that I have n't looked for anything, and that I don't intend to without the full knowledge of that d——d fool who owns the ship."

"You've changed your mind since you wrote that letter," said Sleight coolly, pro-

12

ducing from a drawer the note already known to the reader. Renshaw mechanically extended his hand to take it. Mr. Sleight dropped the letter back into the drawer, which he quietly locked. The apparently simple act dyed Mr. Renshaw's cheek with color, but it vanished quickly, and with it any token of his previous embarrassment. He looked at Sleight with the convinced air of a resolute man who had at last taken a disagreeable step but was willing to stand by the consequences.

"I *have* changed my mind," he said coolly. "I found out that it was one thing to go down there as a skilled prospector might go to examine a mine that was to be valued according to his report of the indications, but that it was entirely another thing to go and play the spy in a poor devil's house in order to buy something he did n't know he was selling and would n't sell if he did."

"And something that the man *he* bought of did n't think of selling; something *he* himself never paid for, and never expected to buy," sneered Sleight.

" But something that *we* expect to buy from our knowledge of all this, and it is that which makes all the difference."

" But you knew all this before."

" I never saw it in this light before! I never thought of it until I was living there face to face with the old fool I was intending to overreach. I never was *sure* of it until this morning, when he actually turned out one of his lodgers that I might have the very room I required to play off our little game in comfortably. When he did that, I made up my mind to drop the whole thing, and I 'm here to do it."

" And let somebody else take the responsibility — with the percentage — unless you 've also felt it your duty to warn Nott too," said Sleight with a sneer.

" You only dare say that to me, Sleight," said Renshaw quietly, " because you have in that drawer an equal evidence of my folly and my confidence ; but if you are wise you will not presume too far on either. Let us see how we stand. Through the yarn of a drunken captain and a mutinous sailor you became aware of an unclaimed shipment of treasure, concealed in an unknown ship that entered this harbor. You are enabled, through me, to corroborate some facts and identify the ship. You proposed to me, as a speculation, to identify the treasure if possible before you purchased the ship. I accepted the offer without consideration ; on consideration I now decline it, but without prejudice or loss to any one but myself. As to your insinuation I need not remind you that my presence here to-day refutes it. I would not require your permission to make a much better bargain with a good natured fool like Nott than I could with you. Or if I did not care for the business I could have warned the girl " —

" The girl — what girl ? "

Renshaw bit his lip but answered boldly.

" The old man's daughter — a poor girl —
whom this act would rob as well as her
father."

Sleight looked at his companion attentively. " You might have said so at first,
and let up on this camp-meetin' exhortation.
Well then — admitting you 've got the old
man and the young girl on the same string,
and that you 've played it pretty low down in
the short time you 've been there — I suppose, Dick Renshaw, I 've got to see your
bluff. Well, how much is it! What 's the
figure you and she have settled on ? "

For an instant Mr. Sleight was in physical danger. But before he had finished
speaking Renshaw's quick sense of the ludicrous had so far overcome his first indignation as to enable him even to admire the
perfect moral insensibility of his companion.
As he rose and walked towards the door, he
half wondered that he had ever treated the
affair seriously. With a smile he replied:

" Far from bluffing, Sleight, I am throw-

ing my cards on the table. Consider that
I've passed out. Let some other man take
my hand. Rake down the pot if you like,
old man, *I* leave for Sacramento to-night.
Adios."

When the door had closed behind him
Mr. Sleight summoned his clerk.

" Is that petition for grading Pontiac
Street ready?"

" I've seen the largest property holders,
sir; they're only waiting for you to sign
first." Mr. Sleight paused and then affixed
his signature to the paper his clerk laid before him. " Get the other names and send
it up at once."

" If Mr. Nott does n't sign, sir?"

" No matter. He will be assessed all the
same." Mr. Sleight took up his hat.

" The Lascar seaman that was here the
other day has been wanting to see you, sir.
I said you were busy."

Mr. Sleight put down his hat. " Send
him up."

Nevertheless Mr. Sleight sat down and at once abstracted himself so completely as to be apparently in utter oblivion of the man who entered. He was lithe and Indian-looking; bearing in dress and manner the careless slouch without the easy frankness of a sailor.

" Well ! " said Sleight without looking up.

" I was only wantin' to know ef you had any news for me, boss ? "

" News ? " echoed Sleight as if absently ; " news of what ? "

" That little matter of the Pontiac we talked about, boss," returned the Lascar with an uneasy servility in the whites of his teeth and eyes.

" Oh," said Sleight, " that's played out. It's a regular fraud. It's an old forecastle yarn, my man, that you can't reel off in the cabin."

The sailor's face darkened.

" The man who was looking into it has thrown the whole thing up. I tell you it's played out!'" repeated Sleight, without raising his head.

" It 's true, boss — every word," said the Lascar, with an appealing insinuation that seemed to struggle hard with savage earnestness. " You can swear me, boss ; I would n't lie to a gentleman like you. Your man has n't half looked, or else — it must be there, or " —

" That 's just it," said Sleight slowly ; " who 's to know that your friends have n't been there already — that seems to have been your style."

" But no one knew it but me, until I told you, I swear to God. I ain't lying, boss, and I ain't drunk. Say — don't give it up, boss. That man of yours likely don't believe it, because he don't know anything about it. I *do* — *I* could find it."

A silence followed. Mr. Sleight remained completely absorbed in his papers for some moments. Then glancing at the Lascar, he took his pen, wrote a hurried note, folded it, addressed it, and, holding it between his fingers, leaned back in his chair.

"If you choose to take this note to my man, he may give it another show. Mind, I don't say that he *will*. He's going to Sacramento to-night, but you could go down there and find him before he starts. He's got a room there, I believe. While you're waiting for him, you might keep your eyes open to satisfy yourself."

"Ay, ay, sir," said the sailor, eagerly endeavoring to catch the eye of his employer. But Mr. Sleight looked straight before him, and he turned to go.

"The Sacramento boat goes at nine," said Mr. Sleight quietly.

This time their glances met, and the Lascar's eye glistened with subtle intelligence. The next moment he was gone, and Mr. Sleight again became absorbed in his papers.

Meanwhile Renshaw was making his way back to the Pontiac with that light-hearted optimism that had characterized his parting with Sleight. It was this quality of his nature, fostered perhaps by the easy civilization in which he moved, that had originally drawn him into relations with the man he just quitted; a quality that had been troubled and darkened by those relations, yet, when they were broken, at once returned. It consequently did not occur to him that he had only selfishly compromised with the difficulty; it seemed to him enough that he had withdrawn from a compact he thought dishonorable; he was not called upon to betray his partner. in that compact merely to benefit others. He had been willing to incur suspicion and loss to reinstate himself in his self-respect, more he could not do without justifying that suspicion. The view taken by Sleight was, after all, that which most business men would take — which even the unbusiness-like Nott would take — which the girl herself might be tempted to listen to. Clearly he could do nothing but abandon the Pontiac and her owner to the fate he could not in honor avert. And even that fate was problematical. It did not follow that the treasure was still concealed in the Pontiac, nor that Nott would be willing to sell her. He would make some excuse to Nott — he smiled to think he would probably be classed in the long line of absconding tenants — he would say good-by to Rosey, and leave for Sacramento that night. He ascended the stairs to the gangway with a freer breast than when he first entered the ship.

Mr. Nott was evidently absent, and after a quick glance at the half-open cabin door, Renshaw turned towards the galley. But Miss Rosey was not in her accustomed haunt, and with a feeling of disappointment, which seemed inconsistent with so slight a cause, he crossed the deck impatiently and entered his room. He was about to close the door when the prolonged rustle of a trailing skirt in the passage attracted his attention. The sound was so unlike that made by any garment worn by Rosey that he remained mo-

tionless, with his hand on the door. The
sound approached nearer, and the next moment a white veiled figure with a trailing
skirt slowly swept past the room. Renshaw's
pulses halted for an instant in half superstitious awe. As the apparition glided on and
vanished in the cabin door he could only see
that it was the form of a beautiful and
graceful woman — but nothing more. Bewildered and curious, he forgot himself so
far as to follow it, and impulsively entered
the cabin. The figure turned, uttered a little cry, threw the veil aside, and showed the
half troubled, half blushing face of Rosey.

" I — beg — your pardon," stammered
Renshaw; " I did n't know it was you."

" I was trying on some things," said Rosey, recovering her composure and pointing
to an open trunk that seemed to contain a
theatrical wardrobe — " some things father
gave me long ago. I wanted to see if there
was anything I could use. I thought I was
all alone in the ship, but fancying I heard a

noise forward I came out to see what it was. I suppose it must have been you."

She raised her clear eyes to his, with a slight touch of womanly reserve that was so incompatible with any vulgar vanity or girlish coquetry that he became the more embarrassed. Her dress, too, of a slightly antique shape, rich but simple, seemed to reveal and accent a certain repose of gentlewomanliness, that he was now wishing to believe he had always noticed. Conscious of a superiority in her that now seemed to change their relations completely, he alone remained silent, awkward, and embarrassed before the girl who had taken care of his room, and who cooked in the galley! What he had thoughtlessly considered a merely vulgar business intrigue against her stupid father, now to his extravagant fancy assumed the proportions of a sacrilege to herself.

"You 've had your revenge, Miss Nott, for the fright I once gave you," he said a little uneasily, "for you quite startled me

just now as you passed. I began to think
the Pontiac was haunted. I thought you
were a ghost. I don't know why such a
ghost should *frighten* anybody," he went on
with a desperate attempt to recover his position by gallantry. "Let me see — that's
Donna Elvira's dress — is it not?"

"I don't think that was the poor woman's
name," said Rosey simply; "she died of
yellow fever at New Orleans as Signora
somebody."

Her ignorance seemed to Mr. Renshaw so
plainly to partake more of the nun than the
provincial that he hesitated to explain to
her that he meant the heroine of an opera.

"It seems dreadful to put on the poor
thing's clothes, does n't it?" she added.

Mr. Renshaw's eyes showed so plainly
that he thought otherwise, that she drew a
little austerely towards the door of her state-
room.

"I must change these things before any
one comes," she said dryly.

"That means I must go, I suppose. But could n't you let me wait here or in the gang-way until then, Miss Nott? I am going away to-night, and I may n't see you again." He had not intended to say this, but it slipped from his embarrassed tongue. She stopped with her hand on the door.

"You are going away?"

"I — think — I must leave to-night. I have some important business in Sacramento."

She raised her frank eyes to his. The unmistakable look of disappointment that he saw in them gave his heart a sudden throb and sent the quick blood to his cheeks.

"It 's too bad," she said, abstractedly. "Nobody ever seems to stay here long. Captain Bower promised to tell me all about the ship and he went away the second week. The photographer left before he finished the picture of the Pontiac; Monsieur de Ferrières has only just gone, and now *you* are going."

"Perhaps, unlike them, I have finished my season of usefulness here," he replied, with a bitterness he would have recalled the next moment. But Rosey, with a faint sigh, saying, " I won't be long," entered the state-room and closed the door behind her

Renshaw bit his lip and pulled at the long silken threads of his moustache until they smarted. Why had he not gone at once? Why was it necessary to say he might not see her again — and if he had said it, why should he add anything more? What was he waiting for now? To endeavor to prove to her that he really bore no resemblance to Captain Bower, the photographer, the crazy Frenchman de Ferrières? Or would he be forced to tell her that he was running away from a conspiracy to defraud her father — merely for something to say? Was there ever such folly? Rosey was " not long," as she had said, but he was beginning to pace the narrow cabin impatiently when the door opened and she returned.

She had resumed her ordinary calico gown, but such was the impression left upon Renshaw's fancy that she seemed to wear it with a new grace. At any other time he might have recognized the change as due to a new corset, which strict veracity compels me to record Rosey had adopted for the first time that morning. Howbeit, her slight coquetry seemed to have passed, for she closed the open trunk with a return of her old listless air, and sitting on it rested her elbows on her knees and her oval chin in her hands.

"I wish you would do me a favor," she said after a reflective pause.

"Let me know what it is and it shall be done," replied Renshaw quickly.

"If you should come across Monsieur de Ferrières, or hear of him, I wish you would let me know. He was very poorly when he left here, and I should like to know if he was better. He did n't say where he was going. At least, he did n't tell father; but I fancy he and father don't agree."

13

" I shall be very glad of having even *that* opportunity of making you remember me, Miss Nott," returned Renshaw with a faint smile; " I don't suppose either that it would be very difficult to get news of your friend — everybody seems to know him."

"But not as I did," said Rosey with an abstracted little sigh.

Mr. Renshaw opened his brown eyes upon her. Was he mistaken? Was this romantic girl only a little coquette playing her provincial airs on him? "You say he and your father did n't agree? That means, I suppose, that *you* and he agreed? — and that was the result."

" I don't think father knew anything about it," said Rosey simply.

Mr. Renshaw rose. And this was what he had been waiting to hear! "Perhaps," he said grimly, "you would also like news of the photographer and Captain Bower, or did your father agree with them better?"

"No," said Rosey quietly. She remained

silent for a moment, and lifting her lashes said, "Father always seemed to agree with *you*, and that " — she hesitated.

"That's why *you* don't."

"I did n't say that," said Rosey with an incongruous increase of coldness and color. "I only meant to say it was that which makes it seem so hard you should go now."

Notwithstanding his previous determination Renshaw found himself sitting down again. Confused and pleased, wishing he had said more — or less — he said nothing, and Rosey was forced to continue.

"It's strange, is n't it — but father was urging me this morning to make a visit to some friends at the old Ranch. I did n't want to go. I like it much better here."

"But you cannot bury yourself here forever, Miss Nott," said Renshaw with a sudden burst of honest enthusiasm. "Sooner or later you will be forced to go where you will be properly appreciated, where you will be admired and courted, where your slightest wish will be law. Believe me, without flattery, you don't know your own power."

"It does n't seem strong enough to keep even the little I like here," said Rosey with a slight glistening of the eyes. "But," she added hastily, "you don't know how much the dear old ship is to me. It's the only home I think I ever had."

"But the Ranch?" said Renshaw.

"The Ranch seemed to be only the old wagon halted in the road. It was a very little improvement on out doors," said Rosey with a little shiver. "But this is so cozy and snug and yet so strange and foreign. Do you know I think I began to understand why I like it so since you taught me so much about ships and voyages. Before that I only learned from books. Books deceive you, I think, more than people do. Don't you think so?"

She evidently did not notice the quick flush that covered his cheeks and apparently dazzled his troubled eyelids, for she went on confidentially.

" I was thinking of you yesterday. I was sitting by the galley door, looking forward. You remember the first day I saw you when you startled me by coming up out of the hatch ? "

" I wish you would n't think of that," said Renshaw, with more earnestness than he would have made apparent.

" *I* don't want to either," said Rosey, gravely, " for I 've had a strange fancy about it. I saw once when I was younger, a picture in a print shop in Montgomery Street that haunted me. I think it was called ' The Pirate.' There was a number of wicked - looking sailors lying around the deck, and coming out of a hatch was one figure with his hands on the' deck and a cutlass in his mouth."

" Thank you," said Renshaw.

" You don't understand. He was horrid-looking, not at all like you. I never thought of *him* when I first saw you ; but the other day I thought how dreadful it would have

been if some one like him and not like you
had come up then. That made me nervous
sometimes of being alone. I think father is
too. He often goes about stealthily at night,
as if hè was watching for something."

Renshaw's face grew suddenly dark.
Could it be possible that Sleight had always
suspected him, and set spies to watch — or
was he guilty of some double intrigue?

"He thinks," continued Rosey with a
faint smile, " that some one is looking around
the ship, and talks of setting bear-traps. I
hope you 're not mad, Mr. Renshaw," she
added, suddenly catching sight of his changed
expression, " at my foolishness in saying
you reminded me of the pirate. I meant
nothing."

"I know you 're incapable of meaning
anything but good to anybody, Miss Nott,
perhaps to me more than I deserve," said
Renshaw with a sudden burst of feeling.
"I wish — I wish — you would do *me* a favor. *You* asked me one just now." He

had taken her hand. It seemed so like a mere illustration of his earnestness, that she did not withdraw it. "Your father tells you everything. If he has any offer to dispose of the ship, will you write to me at once before anything is concluded?" He winced a little — the sentence of Sleight, "What's the figure you and she have settled upon?" flashed across his mind. He scarcely noticed that Rosey had withdrawn her hand coldly.

"Perhaps you had better speak to father, as it is *his* business. Besides, I shall not be here. I shall be at the Ranch."

"But you said you did n't want to go?"

"I 've changed my mind," said Rosey listlessly. "I shall go to-night."

She rose as if to indicate that the interview was ended. With an overpowering instinct that his whole future happiness depended upon his next act, he made a step towards her, with eager outstretched hands. But she slightly lifted her own with a warning gesture, " I hear father coming — you will have a chance to talk *business* with him," she said, and vanished into her state-room.

VI.

The heavy tread of Abner Nott echoed in the passage. Confused and embarrassed, Renshaw remained standing at the door that had closed upon Rosey as her father entered the cabin. Providence, which always fostered Mr. Nott's characteristic misconceptions, left that perspicacious parent but one interpretation of the situation. Rosey had evidently just informed Mr. Renshaw that she loved another !

" I was just saying 'good - by' to Miss Nott," said Renshaw, hastily regaining his composure with an effort. " I am going to Sacramento to-night, and will not return. I " —

" In course, in course," interrupted Nott,

soothingly; "that's wot you say now, and that's what you allow to do. That's wot they allus do."

"I mean," said Renshaw, reddening at what he conceived to be an allusion to the absconding propensities of Nott's previous tenants, — "I mean that you shall keep the advance to cover any loss you might suffer through my giving up the rooms."

"Certingly," said Nott, laying his hand with a large sympathy on Renshaw's shoulder; "but we'll drop that just now. We won't swap hosses in the middle of the river. We'll square up accounts in your room," he added, raising his voice that Rosey might overhear him, after a preliminary wink at the young man. "Yes, sir, we'll just square up and settle in there. Come along, Mr. Renshaw." Pushing him with paternal gentleness from the cabin, with his hand still upon his shoulder, he followed him into the passage. Half annoyed at his familiarity, yet not altogether displeased by this illustration of Rosey's belief of his preference, Renshaw wonderingly accompanied him. Nott closed the door, and pushing the young man into a chair, deliberately seated himself at the table opposite. "It's just as well that Rosey reckons that you and me is settlin' our accounts," he began, cunningly, "and mebbee it's just ez well ez she should reckon you're goin' away."

"But I *am* going," interrupted Renshaw, impatiently. "I leave to-night."

"Surely, surely," said Nott, gently, "that's wot you kalkilate to do; that's just nat'ral in a young feller. That's about what I reckon *I'd* hev done to her mother if anythin' like this hed ever cropped up, which it didn't. Not but what Almiry Jane had young fellers enough round her, but, 'cept ole Judge Peter, ez was lamed in the War of 1812, there ain't no similarity ez I kin see," he added, musingly.

"I am afraid I can't see any similarity either, Mr. Nott," said Renshaw, struggling between a dawning sense of some impending absurdity and his growing passion for Rosey. "For Heaven's sake speak out if you've got anything to say."

Mr. Nott leaned forward, and placed his large hand on the young man's shoulder. "That's it. That's what I sed to myself when I seed how things were pintin'. 'Speak out,' sez I, 'Abner! Speak out if you've got anything to say. You kin trust this yer Mr. Renshaw. He ain't the kind of man to creep into the bosom of a man's ship for pupposes of his own. He ain't a man that would hunt round until he discovered a poor man's treasure, and then try to rob'"—

"Stop!" said Renshaw, with a set face and darkening eyes. "*What* treasure? *what* man are you speaking of?"

"Why Rosey and Mr. Ferrers," returned Nott, simply.

Renshaw sank into his seat again. But the expression of relief which here passed swiftly over his face gave way to one of uneasy interest as Nott went on.

" P'r'aps it 's a little high falutin' talkin' of Rosey ez a treasure. But, considerin', Mr. Renshaw, ez she 's the only prop'ty I 've kept by me for seventeen years ez hez paid interest and increased in valooe, it ain't sayin' too much to call her so. And ez Ferrers knows this, he oughter been content with gougin' me in that horse-hair spec, without goin' for Rosey. P'r'aps yer surprised at hearing me speak o' my own flesh and blood ez if I was talkin' hoss-trade, but you and me is bus'ness men, Mr. Renshaw, and we discusses ez such. We ain't goin' to slosh round and slop over in po'try and sentiment," continued Nott, with a tremulous voice, and a hand that slightly shook on Renshaw's shoulder. " We ain't goin' to git up and sing, ' Thou 'st larned to love another thou 'st broken every vow we 've parted from each other and my bozom 's lonely now oh is it well to sever such hearts as ourn for ever kin I forget thee never farewell farewell farewell.' Ye never happen'd to hear Jim Baker sing that at the moosic hall on Dupont Street, Mr. Renshaw," continued Mr. Nott, enthusiastically, when he had recovered from that complete absence of punctuation which alone suggested verse to his intellect. " He sorter struck water down here," indicating his heart, " every time."

" But what has Miss Nott to do with M. de Ferrières ? " asked Renshaw, with a faint smile.

Mr. Nott regarded him with dumb, round, astonished eyes. " Hez n't she told yer ? "

" Certainly not."

" And she did n't let on anythin' about him ? " he continued, feebly.

" She said she 'd liked to know where " — He stopped, with the reflection that he was betraying her confidences.

A dim foreboding of some new form of deceit, to which even the man before him was a consenting party, almost paralyzed

Nott's faculties. "Then she did n't tell yer that she and Ferrers was sparkin' and keepin' kimpany together; that she and him was engaged, and was kalkilatin' to run away to furrin parts; that she cottoned to him more than to the ship or her father?"

"She certainly did not, and I should n't believe it," said Renshaw, quickly.

Nott smiled. He was amused; he astutely recognized the usual trustfulness of love and youth. There was clearly no deceit here! Renshaw's attentive eyes saw the smile, and his brow darkened.

"I like to hear yer say that, Mr. Renshaw," said Nott, "and it's no more than Rosey deserves, ez it's suthing onnat'ral and spell-like that's come over her through Ferrers. It ain't my Rosey. But it's Gospel truth, whether she's bewitched or not; whether it's them damn fool stories she reads — and it's like ez not he's just the kind o' snipe to write 'em hisself, and sorter advertise hisself, don't yer see — she's allus stuck up for him. They 've had clandesent interviews, and when I taxed him with it he ez much ez allowed it was so, and reckoned he must leave, so ez he could run her off, you know — kinder stampede her with 'honor.' Them 's his very words."

" But that is all past; he is gone, and Miss Nott does not even know where he is!" said Renshaw, with a laugh, which, however, concealed a vague uneasiness.

Mr. Nott rose and opened the door carefully. When he had satisfied himself that no one was listening, he came back and said in a whisper, "That 's a lie. Not ez Rosey means to lie, but it 's a trick he 's put upon that poor child. That man, Mr. Renshaw, hez been hangin' round the Pontiac ever since. I 've seed him twice with my own eyes pass the cabin windys. More than that, I 've heard strange noises at night, and seen strange faces in the alley over yer. And only jist now ez I kem in I ketched sight of a furrin lookin' Chinee nigger slinking round the back door of what useter be Ferrers's loft."

"Did he look like a sailor?" asked Renshaw quickly, with a return of his former suspicion.

"Not more than I do," said Nott, glancing complacently at his pea-jacket. "He had rings on his yeers like a wench."

Mr. Renshaw started. But seeing Nott's eyes fixed on him, he said lightly, "But what have these strange faces and this strange man — probably only a Lascar sailor out of a job — to do with Ferrières?"

"Friends o' his — feller furrin citizens — spies on Rosey, don't you see? But they can't play the old man, Mr. Renshaw. I 've told Rosey she must make a visit to the old Ranch. Once I 've got her ther safe, I reckon I kin manage Mr. Ferrers and any number of Chinee niggers he kin bring along."

Renshaw remained for a few moments lost in thought. Then rising suddenly he grasped Mr. Nott's hand with a frank smile but determined eyes. "I have n't got the hang of this, Mr. Nott — the whole thing gets me! I only know that I 've changed my mind. I 'm *not* going to Sacramento. I shall stay *here*, old man, until I see you safe through the business, or my name 's not Dick Renshaw. There 's my hand on it! Don't say a word. Maybe it is no more than I ought to do — perhaps not half enough. Only remember, not a word of this to your daughter. She must believe that I leave to-night. And the sooner you get her out of this cursed ship the better."

"Deacon Flint's girls are goin' up in to-night's boat. I 'll send Rosey with them," said Nott with a cunning twinkle. Renshaw nodded. Nott seized his hand with a wink of unutterable significance.

Left to himself Renshaw tried to review more calmly the circumstances in these strange revelations that had impelled him to change his resolution so suddenly. That the ship was under the surveillance of unknown parties, and that the description of them tallied with his own knowledge of a certain Lascar sailor, who was one of Sleight's informants — seemed to be more than probable. That this seemed to point to Sleight's disloyalty to himself while he was acting as his agent, or a double treachery on the part of Sleight's informants, was in either case a reason and an excuse for his own interference. But the connection of the absurd Frenchman with the case, which at first seemed a characteristic imbecility of his landlord, bewildered him the more he thought of it. Rejecting any hypothesis of the girl's affection for the antiquated figure whose sanity was a question of public criticism, he was forced to the equally alarming theory that Ferrières was cognizant of the treasure, and that his attentions to Rosey were to gain possession of it by marrying her. Might she not be dazzled by a picture of this wealth? Was is not possible that she was already in part possession of the

secret, and her strange attraction to the ship,
and what he had deemed her innocent craving for information concerning it, a conse-
quence? Why had he not thought of this
before? Perhaps she had detected his purpose from the first, and had deliberately
checkmated him. The thought did not increase his complacency as Nott softly returned.

"It's all right," he began with a certain
satisfaction in this rare opportunity for
Machiavellian diplomacy, "it's all fixed now.
Rosey tumbled to it at once, partiklerly when
I said you was bound to go. 'But wot
makes Mr. Renshaw go, father,' sez she;
'wot makes everybody run away from the
ship?' sez she, rather peart like and sassy
for her. 'Mr. Renshaw hez contractin' business,' sez I; 'got a big thing up in Sacramento that 'll make his fortun',' sez I — for
I was n't goin' to give yer away, don't ye see.
'He had some business to talk to you about
the ship,' sez she, lookin' at me under the

corner of her pocket handkerchief. ' Lots o' business,' sez I. ' Then I reckon he don't care to hev me write to him,' sez she. ' Not a bit,' sez I, ' he would n't answer ye if ye did. Ye 'll never hear from that chap agin.' "

" But what the devil " — interrupted the young man impetuously.

"Keep yer hair on! " remonstrated the old man with dark intelligence. " Ef you 'd seen the way she flounced into her state room! — she, Rosey, ez allus moves ez softly ez a spirit — you 'd hev wished I 'd hev unloaded a little more. No sir, gals is gals in some things all the time."

Renshaw rose and paced the room rapidly. " Perhaps I 'd better speak to her again be-before she goes," he said, impulsively.

" P'r'aps you 'd better not," replied the imperturbable Nott.

Irritated as he was, Renshaw could not avoid the reflection that the old man was right. What, indeed, could he say to her with his present imperfect knowledge? How could she write to him if that knowledge was correct?

" Ef," said Nott, kindly, with a laying on of large benedictory and paternal hands, " ef yer are willin' to see Rosey agin, without *speakin'* to her, I reckon I ken fix it for yer. I 'm goin' to take her down to the boat in half an hour. Ef yer should happen — mind, ef yer should *happen* to be down there, seein' some friends off and sorter promenadin' up and down the wharf like them high-toned chaps on Montgomery Street — ye might ketch her eye unconscious like. Or, ye might do this ! " He rose after a moment's cogitation and with a face of profound mystery opened the door and beckoned Renshaw to follow him. Leading the way cautiously, he brought the young man into an open unpartitioned recess beside her state room. It seemed to be used as a store room, and Renshaw's eye was caught by a trunk the size and shape of the one that had provided Rosey with the materials of her mas-

querade. Pointing to it Mr. Nott said in
a grave whisper: " This yer trunk is the
companion trunk to Rosey's. *She's* got the
things them opery women wears; this yer
contains the *he* things, the duds and fixin's
o' the men o' the same stripe." Throwing
it open he continued : " Now, Mr. Renshaw,
gals is gals; it 's nat'ral they should be took
by fancy dress and store clothes on young
chaps as on theirselves. That man Ferrers
hez got the dead wood on all of ye in this
sort of thing, and hez been playing, so to
speak, a lone hand all along. And ef thar 's
anythin' in thar," he added, lifting part of
a theatrical wardrobe, " that you think you 'd
fancy — anythin' you 'd like to put on when
ye promenade the wharf down yonder — it 's
yours. Don't ye be bashful, but help yourself."

It was fully a minute before Renshaw
fairly grasped the old man's meaning. But
when he did — when the suggested spectacle
of himself arrayed *à la* Ferrières, gravely

promenading the wharf as a last gorgeous
appeal to the affections of Rosey, rose before his fancy, he gave way to a fit of genuine laughter. The nervous tension of the
past few hours relaxed; he laughed until
the tears came into his eyes; he was still
laughing when the door of the cabin was
suddenly opened and Rosey appeared cold
and distant on the threshold.

"I — beg your pardon," stammered Renshaw hastily. "I did n't mean — to disturb
you — I " —

Without looking at him Rosey turned to
her father. "I am ready," she said coldly,
and closed the door again.

A glance of artful intelligence came into
Nott's eyes, which had remained blankly
staring at Renshaw's apparently causeless
hilarity. Turning to him he winked sol-
emnly. "That keerless kind o' hoss-laff
jist fetched her," he whispered, and vanished before his chagrined companion could
reply.

When Mr. Nott and his daughter departed Renshaw was not in the ship, neither did he make a spectacular appearance on the wharf as Mr. Nott had fondly expected, nor did he turn up again until after nine o'clock, when he found the old man in the cabin awaiting his return with some agitation. " A minit ago," he said, mysteriously closing the door behind Renshaw, " I heard a voice in the passage, and goin' out who should I see agin but that darned furrin nigger ez I told yer 'bout, kinder hidin' in the dark, his eyes shinin' like a catamount. I was jist reachin' for my weppins when he riz up with a grin and handed me this yer letter. I told him I reckoned you 'd gone to Sacramento, but he said he wez sure you was in your room, and to prove it I went thar. But when I kem back the d——d skunk had vamoosed — got frightened I reckon — and was n't nowhar to be seen."

Renshaw took the letter hastily. It contained only a line in Sleight's hand. " If you change your mind, the bearer may be of service to you."

He turned abruptly to Nott. "You say it was the same Lascar you saw before?"

"It was."

"Then all I can say is he is no agent of de Ferrières's," said Renshaw, turning away with a disappointed air. Mr. Nott would have asked another question, but with an abrupt "Good-night" the young man entered his room, locked the door, and threw himself on his bed to reflect without interruption.

But if he was in no mood to stand Nott's fatuous conjectures, he was less inclined to be satisfied with his own. Had he been again carried away through his impulses evoked by the caprices of a pretty coquette and the absurd theories of her half imbecile father? Had he broken faith with Sleight and remained in the ship for nothing, and would not his change of resolution appear to be the result of Sleight's note? But why

had the Lascar been haunting the ship before? In the midst of these conjectures he
fell asleep.

VII.

Between three and four in the morning
the clouds broke over the Pontiac, and the
moon, riding high, picked out in black and
silver the long hulk that lay cradled between
the iron shells of warehouses and the wooden
frames of tenements on either side. The
galley and covered gangway presented a
mass of undefined shadow, against which the
white deck shone brightly, stretching to the
forecastle and bows, where the tiny glass
roof of the photographer glistened like a
gem in the Pontiac's crest. So peaceful and
motionless she lay that she might have been
some petrifaction of a past age now first ex-
humed and laid bare to the cold light of the
stars.

Nevertheless this calm security was presently invaded by a sense of stealthy life and motion. What had seemed a fixed shadow suddenly detached itself from the deck, and began to slip stanchion by stanchion along the bulwarks toward the companion way. At the cabin door it halted and crouched motionless. Then rising, it glided forward with the same staccato movement until opposite the slight elevation of the forehatch. Suddenly it darted to the hatch, unfastened and lifted it with a swift, familiar dexterity, and disappeared in the opening. But as the moon shone upon its vanishing face, it revealed the whitening eyes and teeth of the Lascar seaman.

Dropping to the lower deck lightly, he felt his way through the dark passage between the partitions, evidently less familiar to him, halting before each door to listen. Returning forward he reached the second hatchway that had attracted Rosey's attention, and noiselessly unclosed its fastenings. A penetrating smell of bilge arose from the opening. Drawing a small bull's-eye lantern from his breast he lit it, and unhesitatingly let himself down to the further depth. The moving flash of his light revealed the recesses of the upper hold, the abyss of the well amidships, and glanced from the shining backs of moving zigzags of rats that seemed to outline the shadowy beams and transoms. Disregarding those curious spectators of his movements, he turned his attention eagerly to the inner casings of the hold, that seemed in one spot to have been strengthened by fresh timbers. Attacking this stealthily with the aid of some tools hidden in his oil-skin clothing, in the light of the lantern he bore a fanciful resemblance to the predatory animals around him. The low continuous sound of rasping and gnawing of timber which followed heightened the resemblance. At the end of a few minutes he had succeeded in removing enough of the outer planking to show that the entire filling of the casing between the stanchions was composed of small boxes. Dragging out one of them with feverish eagerness to the light, the Lascar forced it open. In the rays of the bull's-eye, a wedged mass of discolored coins show with a lurid glow. The story of the Pontiac was true — the treasure was there!

But Mr. Sleight had overlooked the logical effect of this discovery on the natural villainy of his tool. In the very moment of his triumphant execution of his patron's suggestions the idea of keeping the treasure to himself flashed upon his mind. *He* had discovered it — why should he give it up to anybody? *He* had run all the risks; if he were detected at that moment, who would believe that his purpose there at midnight was only to satisfy some one else that the treasure was still intact? No. The circumstances were propitious; he would get the treasure out of the ship at once, drop it over her side, hastily conceal it in the nearest lot adjacent, and take it away at his convenience. — Who would be the wiser for it?

But it was necessary to reconnoitre first. He knew that the loft overhead was empty. He knew that it communicated with the alley, for he hád tried the door that morning. He would convey the treasure there, and drop it into the alley. The boxes were heavy. Each one would require a separate journey to the ship's side, but he would at least secure something if he were interrupted. He stripped the casing, and gathered the boxes together in a pile.

Ah, yes, it was funny too that he — the Lascar hound — the d——d nigger — should get what bigger and bullier men than he had died for! The mate's blood was on those boxes, if the salt water had not washed it out. It was a hell of a fight when they dragged the captain — Oh, what was that? Was it the splash of a rat in the bilge, or what?

A superstitious terror had begun to seize

him at the thought of blood. The stifling
hold seemed again filled with struggling figures he had known; the air thick with cries
and blasphemies that he had forgotten. He
rose to his feet, and running quickly to the
hatchway, leaped to the deck above. All
was quiet. The door leading to the empty
loft yielded to his touch. He entered, and,
gliding through, unbarred and opened the
door that gave upon the alley. The cold
air and moonlight flowed in silently; the
way of escape was clear. Bah! He would
go back for the treasure.

He had reached the passage when the
door he had just opened was suddenly darkened. Turning rapidly, he was conscious of
a gaunt figure, grotesque, silent, and erect,
looming on the threshold between him and
the sky. Hidden in the shadow, he made a
stealthy step towards it, with an iron wrench
in his uplifted hand. But the next moment
his eyes dilated with superstitious horror;
the iron fell from his hand, and with a

scream, like a frightened animal, he turned
and fled into the passage. In the first access
of his blind terror he tried to reach the deck
above through the forehatch, but was stopped
by the sound of a heavy tread overhead.
The immediate fear of detection now over-
came his superstition; he would have even
faced the apparition again to escape through
the loft; but, before he could return there,
other footsteps approached rapidly from the
end of the passage he would have to trav-
erse. There was but one chance of escape
left now — the forehold he had just quitted.
He might hide there until the alarm was
over. He glided back to the hatch, lifted
it, and it closed softly over his head as the
upper hatch was simultaneously raised, and
the small round eyes of Abner Nott peered
down upon it. The other footsteps proved
to be Renshaw's, but, attracted by the open
door of the loft, he turned aside and entered.
As soon as he disappeared Mr. Nott cautiously dropped through the opening to the

deck below, and, going to the other hatch through which the Lascar had vanished, deliberately refastened it. In a few moments Renshaw returned with a light, and found the old man sitting on the hatch.

"The loft door was open," said Renshaw "There's little doubt whoever was here escaped that way."

"Surely," said Nott. There was a peculiar look of Machiavellian sagacity in his face which irritated Renshaw.

"Then you're sure it was Ferrières you saw pass by your window before you called me?" he asked.

Nott nodded his head with an expression of infinite profundity.

"But you say he was going *from* the ship. Then it could not have been he who made the noise we heard down here."

"Mebbee no, and mebbee yes," returned Nott, cautiously.

"But if he was already concealed inside the ship, as that open door, which you say

15

you barred from the inside, would indicate, what the devil did he want with this?" said Renshaw, producing the monkey-wrench he had picked up.

Mr. Nott examined the tool carefully, and shook his head with momentous significance. Nevertheless, his eyes wandered to the hatch on which he was seated.

"Did you find anything disturbed *there?*" said Renshaw, following the direction of his eye. "Was that hatch fastened as it is now?"

"It was," said Nott, calmly. "But ye would n't mind fetchin' me a hammer and some o' them big nails from the locker, would yer, while I hang round here just so ez to make sure against another attack."

Renshaw complied with his request; but as Nott proceeded to gravely nail down the fastenings of the hatch, he turned impatiently away to complete his examination of the ship. The doors of the other lofts and their fastenings appeared secure and undisturbed.

Yet it was undeniable that a felonious entrance had been made, but, by whom or for what purpose, still remained uncertain. Even now, Renshaw found it difficult to accept Nott's theory that de Ferrières was the aggressor and Rosey the object, nor could he justify his own suspicion that the Lascar had obtained a surreptitious entrance under Sleight's directions. With a feeling that if Rosey had been present he would have confessed all, and demanded from her an equal confidence, he began to hate his feeble, purposeless, and inefficient alliance with her father, who believed but dare not tax his daughter with complicity in this outrage. What could be done with a man whose only idea of action at such a moment was to nail up an undisturbed entrance in his invaded house! He was so preoccupied with these thoughts that when Nott rejoined him in the cabin he scarcely heeded his presence, and was entirely oblivious of the furtive looks which the old man from time to time cast upon his face.

"I reckon ye would n't mind," broke in Nott, suddenly, "ef I asked a favor of ye, Mr. Renshaw. Mebbee ye 'll allow it 's askin' too much in the matter of expense; mebbee ye 'll allow it 's askin' too much in the matter o' time. But *I* kalkilate to pay all the expense, and if you 'd let me know what yer vally yer time at, I reckon I could stand that. What I 'd be askin' is this. Would ye mind takin' a letter from me to Rosey, and bringin' back an answer?"

Renshaw stared speechlessly at this absurd realization of his wish of a moment before. "I don't think I understand you," he stammered.

"P'r'aps not," returned Nott, with great gravity. "But that 's not so much matter to you ez your time and expenses."

"I meant I should be glad to go if I can be of any service to you," said Renshaw, hastily.

"You kin ketch the seven o'clock boat this morning, and you 'll reach San Rafael at ten" —

"But I thought Miss Rosey went to Petaluma," interrupted Renshaw quickly.

Nott regarded him with an expression of patronizing superiority. "That's what we ladled out to the public gin'rally, and to Ferrers and his gang in partickler. We *said* Petalumey, but if you go to Madroño Cottage, San Rafael, you'll find Rosey thar."

If Mr. Renshaw required anything more to convince him of the necessity of coming to some understanding with Rosey at once it would have been this last evidence of her father's utterly dark and supremely inscrutable designs. He assented quickly, and Nott handed him a note.

"Ye'll be partickler to give this inter her own hands, and wait for an answer," said Nott gravely.

Resisting the proposition to enter then and there into an elaborate calculation of the value of his time and the expenses of the trip, Renshaw found himself at seven o'clock on the San Rafael boat. Brief as was the journey it gave him time to reflect upon his coming interview with Rosey. He had resolved to begin by confessing all; the attempt of last night had released him from any sense of duty to Sleight. Besides, he did not doubt that Nott's letter contained some reference to this affair only known to Nott's dark and tortuous intelligence.

VIII.

Madroño Cottage lay at the entrance of a little *cañada* already green with the early winter rains, and nestled in a thicket of the harlequin painted trees that gave it a name. The young man was a little relieved to find that Rosey had gone to the post-office a mile away, and that he would probably overtake her or meet her returning — alone. The road — little more than a trail — wound along the crest of the hill looking across the *cañada* to the long, dark, heavily-wooded flank of

Mount Tamalpais that rose from the valley a dozen miles away. A cessation of the warm rain, a rift in the sky, and the rare spectacle of cloud scenery, combined with a certain sense of freedom, restored that light-hearted gayety that became him most. At a sudden turn of the road he caught sight of Rosey's figure coming towards him, and quickened his step with the impulsiveness of of a boy. But she suddenly disappeared, and when he again saw her she was on the other side of the trail apparently picking the leaves of a manzanita. She had already seen him.

Somehow the frankness of his greeting was checked. She looked up at him with cheeks that retained enough of their color to suggest why she had hesitated, and said, " *You* here, Mr. Renshaw? I thought you were in Sacramento."

" And I thought *you* were in Petaluma," he retorted gayly. " I have a letter from your father. The fact is, one of those gentlemen who has been haunting the ship actually made an entry last night. Who he was, and what he came for, nobody knows. Perhaps your father gives you his suspicions." He could not help looking at her narrowly as he handed her the note. Except that her pretty eyebrows were slightly raised in curiosity she seemed undisturbed as she opened the letter. Presently she raised her eyes to his.

"Is this all father gave you?"

"All."

"You're sure you haven't dropped anything?"

"Nothing. I have given you all he gave me."

"And that is all it is." She exhibited the missive, a perfectly blank sheet of paper folded like a note!

Renshaw felt the angry blood glow in his cheeks. "This is unpardonable! I assure you, Miss Nott, there must be some mistake. He himself has probably forgotten the inclosure," he continued, yet with an inward conviction that the act was perfectly premeditated on the part of the old man.

The young girl held out her hand frankly. "Don't think any more of it, Mr. Renshaw. Father is forgetful at times. But tell me about last night."

In a few words Mr. Renshaw briefly but plainly related the details of the attempt upon the Pontiac, from the moment that he had been awakened by Nott, to his discovery of the unknown trespasser's flight by the open door to the loft. When he had finished, he hesitated, and then taking Rosey's hand, said impulsively, "You will not be angry with me if I tell you all? Your father firmly believes that the attempt was made by the old Frenchman, de Ferrières, with a view of carrying you off."

A dozen reasons other than the one her father would have attributed it to might have called the blood to her face. But only innocence could have brought the look of astonished indignation to her eyes as she answered quickly :

"So *that* was what you were laughing at?"

"Not that, Miss Nott," said the young man eagerly: "though I wish to God I could accuse myself of nothing more disloyal. Do not speak, I beg," he added impatiently, as Rosey was about to reply. " I have no right to hear you ; I have no right to even stand in your presence until I have confessed everything. I came to the Pontiac ; I made your acquaintance, Miss Nott, through a fraud as wicked as anything your father charges to de Ferrières. I am not a contractor. I never was an honest lodger in the Pontiac. I was simply a spy."

"But you did n't mean to be — it was some mistake, was n't it? " said Rosey, quite white, but more from sympathy with the offender's emotion than horror at the offense.

" I am afraid I did mean it. But bear with me for a few moments longer and you

shall know all. It's a long story. Will you
walk on, and — take my arm ? You do not
shrink from me, Miss Nott. Thank you. I
scarcely deserve the kindness."

Indeed so little did Rosey shrink that he
was conscious of a slight reassuring pressure
on his arm as they moved forward, and for
the moment I fear the young man felt like
exaggerating his offense for the sake of pro-
portionate sympathy. " Do you remember,"
he continued, " one evening when I told you
some sea tales, you said you always thought
there must be some story about the Pontiac ?
There *was* a story of the Pontiac, Miss Nott
— a wicked story — a terrible story — which
I might have told you, which I *ought* to
have told you — which was the story that
brought me there. You were right, too, in
saying that you thought I had known the
Pontiac before I stepped first on her deck
that day. I had."

He laid his disengaged hand across lightly
on Rosey's, as if to assure himself that she
was listening.

" I was at that time a sailor. I had been
fool enough to run away from college, thinking it a fine romantic thing to ship before the
mast for a voyage round the world. I was a
little disappointed, perhaps, but I made the
best of it, and in two years I was the second
mate of a whaler lying in a little harbor of
one of the uncivilized islands of the Pacific.
While we were at anchor there a French
trading vessel put in, apparently for water.
She had the dregs of a mixed crew of Las-
cars and Portuguese, who said they had lost
the rest of their men by desertion, and that
the captain and mate had been carried off
by fever. There was something so queer in
their story that our skipper took the law in
his own hands, and put me on board of her
with a salvage crew. But that night the
French crew mutinied, cut the cables, and
would have got to sea if we had not been
armed and prepared, and managed to drive
them below. When we had got them under
hatches for a few hours they parleyed, and

offered to go quietly ashore. As we were short of hands and unable to take them with us, and as we had no evidence against them, we let them go, took the ship to Callao, turned her over to the authorities, lodged a claim for salvage, and continued our voyage. When we returned we found the truth of the story was known. She had been a French trader from Marseilles, owned by her captain ; her crew had mutinied in the Pacific, killed their officers and the only passenger — the owner of the cargo. They had made away with the cargo and a treasure of nearly half a million of Spanish gold for trading purposes which belonged to the passenger. In course of time the ship was sold for salvage and put into the South American trade until the breaking out of the Californian gold excitement, when she was sent with a cargo to San Francisco. That ship was the Pontiac which your father bought."

A slight shudder ran through the girl's frame. "I wish — I wish you had n't told me," she said. "I shall never close my eyes again comfortably on board of her, I know."

"I would say that you had purified her of *all* stains of her past — but there may be one that remains. And *that* in most people's eyes would be no detraction. You look puzzled, Miss Nott — but I am coming to the explanation and the end of my story. A ship of war was sent to the island to punish the mutineers and pirates, for such they were, but they could not be found. A private expedition was sent to discover the treasure which they were supposed to have buried, but in vain. About two months ago Mr. Sleight told me one of his shipmasters had sent him a Lascar sailor who had to dispose of a valuable secret regarding the Pontiac for a percentage. That secret was that the treasure was never taken by the mutineers out of the Pontiac! They were about to land and bury it when we boarded them. They took advantage of their imprisonment under hatches *to bury it in the ship.* They hid it in the hold so securely and safely that it was never detected by us or the Callao authorities. I was then asked, as one who knew the vessel, to undertake a private examination of her, with a view of purchasing her from your father without awakening his suspicions. I assented. You have my confession now, Miss Nott. You know my crime. I am at your mercy."

Rosey's arm only tightened around his own. Her eyes sought his. " And you did n't find anything?" she said.

The question sounded so oddly like Sleight's, that Renshaw returned a little stiffly —

" I did n't look."

" Why ? " asked Rosey simply.

" Because," stammered Renshaw, with an uneasy consciousness of having exaggerated his sentiment, " it did n't seem honorable ; it did n't seem fair to you."

" Oh you silly! you might have looked and told *me.*"

"But," said Renshaw, "do you think that would have been fair to Sleight?"

"As fair to him as to us. For, don't you see, it would n't belong to any of us. It would belong to the friends or the family of the man who lost it."

"But there were no heirs," replied Renshaw. "That was proved by some impostor who pretended to be his brother, and libelled the Pontiac at Callao, but the courts decided he was a lunatic."

"Then it belongs to the poor pirates who risked their own lives for it, rather than to Sleight, who did nothing." She was silent for a moment, and then resumed with energy, "I believe he was at the bottom of that attack last night."

"I have thought so too," said Renshaw.

"Then I must go back at once," she continued impulsively. "Father must not be left alone."

"Nor must *you*," said Renshaw, quickly. "Do let me return with you, and share with you and your father the trouble I have brought upon you. Do not," he added in a lower tone, " deprive me of the only chance of expiating my offense, of making myself worthy your forgiveness."

" I am sure," said Rosey, lowering her lids and half withdrawing her arm, " I am sure I have nothing to forgive. You did not believe the treasure belonged to us any more than to anybody else, until you knew *me* " —

"That is true," said the young man, attempting to take her hand.

" I mean," said Rosey, blushing, and showing a distracting row of little teeth in one of her infrequent laughs, " oh, you know what I mean." She withdrew her arm gently, and became interested in the selection of certain wayside bay leaves as they passed along. " All the same, I don't believe in this treasure," she said abruptly, as if to change the subject. " I don't believe it ever was hidden inside the Pontiac."

16

"That can easily be ascertained now," said Renshaw.

"But it's a pity you did n't find it out while you were about it," said Rosey. "It would have saved so much talk and trouble."

"I have told you why I did n't search the ship," responded Renshaw, with a slight bitterness. "But it seems I could only avoid being a great rascal by becoming a great fool."

"You never intended to be a rascal," said Rosey, earnestly, "and you could n't be a fool, except in heeding what a silly girl says. I only meant if you had taken me into your confidence it would have been better."

"Might I not say the same to you regarding your friend, the old Frenchman?" returned Renshaw. "What if I were to confess to you that I lately suspected him of knowing the secret, and of trying to gain your assistance?"

Instead of indignantly repudiating the suggestion, to the young man's great discomfiture, Rosy only knit her pretty brows, and remained for some moments silent. Presently she asked timidly, —

"Do you think it wrong to tell another person's secret for their own good?"

"No," said Renshaw, promptly.

"Then I 'll tell you Monsieur de Ferrières's! But only because I believe from what you have just said that he will turn out to have some right to the treasure."

Then with kindling eyes, and a voice eloquent with sympathy, Rosey told the story of her accidental discovery of de Ferrières's miserable existence in the loft. Clothing it with the unconscious poetry of her fresh, young imagination, she lightly passed over his antique gallantry and grotesque weakness, exalting only his lonely sufferings and mysterious wrongs. Renshaw listened, lost between shame for his late suspicions and admiration for her thoughtful delicacy, until she began to speak of de Ferrières's strange allusions to the foreign papers in his portmanteau. " I think some were law papers, and I am almost certain I saw the word Callao printed on one of them."

" It may be so," said Renshaw, thoughtfully. " The old Frenchman has always passed for a harmless, wandering eccentric. I hardly think public curiosity has ever even sought to know his name, much less his history. But had we not better first try to find if there *is* any property before we examine his claims to it ? "

" As you please," said Rosey, with a slight pout; " but you will find it much easier to discover him than his treasure. It 's always easier to find the thing you 're not looking for."

" Until you want it," said Renshaw, with sudden gravity.

" How pretty it looks over there," said Rosey, turning her conscious eyes to the opposite mountain.

" Very."

They had reached the top of the hill, and in the near distance the chimney of Madroño Cottage was even now visible. At the expected sight they unconsciously stopped — unconsciously disappointed. Rosey broke the embarrassing silence.

"There's another way home, but it's a roundabout way," she said timidly.

"Let us take it," said Renshaw.

She hesitated. "The boat goes at four, and we must return to-night."

"The more reason why we should make the most of our time now," said Renshaw with a faint smile. "To-morrow all things may be changed; to-morrow you may find yourself an heiress, Miss Nott. To-morrow," he added, with a slight tremor in his voice, "I may have earned your forgiveness, only to say farewell to you forever. Let me keep this sunshine, this picture, this companionship with you long enough to say now what perhaps I must not say to-morrow."

They were silent for a moment, and then

by a common instinct turned together into a
narrow trail, scarce wide enough fo. two,
that diverged from the straight practical
path before them. It was indeed a roundabout way home, so roundabout, in fact,
that as they wandered on it seemed even
to double on its track, occasionally lingering long and becoming indistinct under the
shadow of madroño and willow; at one time
stopping blindly before a fallen tree in the
hollow, where they had quite lost it, and
had to sit down to recall it; a rough way,
often requiring the mutual help of each
other's hands and eyes to tread together in
security; an uncertain way, not to be found
without whispered consultation and concession, and yet a way eventually bringing them
hand in hand, happy and hopeful, to the
gate of Madroño Cottage. And if there
was only just time for Rosey to prepare to
take the boat, it was due to the deviousness
of the way. If a stray curl was lying loose
on Rosey's cheek, and a long hair had caught

in Renshaw's button, it was owing to the roughness of the way ; and if in the tones of their voices and in the glances of their eyes there was a maturer seriousness, it was due to the dim uncertainty of the path they had traveled, and would hereafter tread together.

IX.

When Mr. Nott had satisfied himself of Renshaw's departure, he coolly bolted the door at the head of the companion way, thus cutting off any communication with the lower deck. Taking a long rifle from the rack above his berth, he carefully examined the hammer and cap, and then cautiously let himself down through the forehatch to the deck below. After a deliberate survey of the still intact fastenings of the hatch over the forehold, he proceeded quietly to unloose them again with the aid of the tools that still lay there. When the hatch was

once more free he lifted it, and, withdrawing a few feet from the opening, sat himself
down, rifle in hand. A profound silence
reigned throughout the lower deck.

"Ye kin rize up out o' that," said Nott
gently.

There was a stealthy rustle below that
seemed to approach the hatch, and then with
a sudden bound the Lascar leaped on the
deck. But at the same instant Nott covered
him with his rifle. A slight shade of disappointment and surprise had crossed the old
man's face, and clouded his small round eyes
at the apparition of the Lascar, but his hand
was none the less firm upon the trigger as
the frightened prisoner sank on his knees,
with his hands clasped in the attitude of
supplication for mercy.

"Ef you 're thinkin' o' skippin' afore I 've
done with yer," said Nott with labored gentleness, " I oughter warn ye that it 's my style
to drop Injins at two hundred yards, and
this deck ain't anywhere more 'n fifty. It 's

an uncomfortable style, a nasty style — but it's *my* style. I thought I'd tell yer, so yer could take it easy where you air. Where's Ferrers?"

Even in the man's insane terror, his utter bewilderment at the question was evident. "Ferrers?" he gasped; "don't know him, I swear to God, boss."

"P'r'aps," said Nott, with infinite cunning, "yer don't know the man ez kem into the loft from the alley last night — p'r'aps yer didn't see an airy Frenchman with a dyed moustache, eh? I thought that would fetch ye!" he continued, as the man started at the evidence that his vision of last night was a living man. "P'r'aps you and him didn't break into this ship last night, jist to run off with my darter Rosey? P'r'aps yer don't know Rosey, eh? P'r'aps yer don't know ez Ferrers wants to marry her, and hez been hangin' round yer ever since he left — eh?"

Scarcely believing the evidence of his senses that the old man whose treasure he had been trying to steal was utterly ignorant of his real offense, and yet uncertain of the penalty of the other crime of which he was accused, the Lascar writhed his body and stammered vaguely, " Mercy ! Mercy ! "

" Well," said Nott, cautiously, " ez I reckon the hide of a dead Chinee nigger ain't any more vallyble than that of a dead Injin, I don't care ef I let up on yer — seein' the cussedness ain't yours. But ef I let yer off this once, you must take a message to Ferrers from me."

" Let me off this time, boss, and I swear to God I will," said the Lascar eagerly.

" Ye kin say to Ferrers — let me see " — deliberated Nott, leaning on his rifle with cautious reflection. " Ye kin say to Ferrers like this — sez you, 'Ferrers,' sez you, 'the old man sez that afore you went away you sez to him, sez you, " I take my honor with me," sez you ' — have you got that ? " interrupted Nott suddenly.

" Yes, boss."

" ' I take my honor with me,' sez you," repeated Nott slowly. " ' Now,' sez you — ' the
old man sez, sez he — tell Ferrers, sez he,
that his honor havin' run away agin, he
sends it back to him, and ef he ever ketches
it around after this, he 'll shoot it on sight.'
Hev yer got that?"

"Yes," stammered the bewildered captive.

"Then git!"

The Lascar sprang to his feet with the
agility of a panther, leaped through the hatch
above him, and disappeared over the bow of
the ship with an unhesitating directness that
showed that every avenue of escape had been
already contemplated by him. Slipping
lightly from the cutwater to the ground, he
continued his flight, only stopping at the
private office of Mr. Sleight.

When Mr. Renshaw and Rosey Nott arrived on board the Pontiac that evening, they
were astonished to find the passage before the
cabin completely occupied with trunks and
boxes, and the bulk of their household goods

apparently in the process of removal. Mr. Nott, who was superintending the work of two Chinamen, betrayed not only no surprise at the appearance of the young people, but not the remotest recognition of their own bewilderment at his occupation.

"Kalkilatin'," he remarked casually to his daughter, "you 'd rather look arter your fixin's, Rosey, I 've left 'em till the last. P'r'aps yer and Mr. Renshaw would n't mind sittin' down on that locker until I've strapped this yer box."

"But what does it all mean father?" said Rosey, taking the old man by the lappels of his pea-jacket, and slightly emphasizing her question. "What in the name of goodness are you doing?"

"Breakin' camp, Rosey dear, breakin' camp, jist ez we uster," replied Nott with cheerful philosophy. "Kinder like ole times, ain't it? Lord, Rosey," he continued, stopping and following up the reminiscence, with the end of the rope in his hand as if it were a clue, "don't ye mind that day we started outer Livermore Pass, and seed the hull o' the Californy coast stretchin' yonder — eh? But don't ye be skeered, Rosey dear," he added quickly, as if in recognition of the alarm expressed in her face. "I ain't turning ye outer house and home; I've jist hired that 'ere Madroño Cottage from the Peters ontil we kin look round."

"But you're not leaving the ship, father," continued Rosey, impetuously. "You haven't sold it to that man Sleight?"

Mr. Nott rose and carefully closed the cabin door. Then drawing a large wallet from his pocket, he said, "It's sing'lar ye should hev got the name right the first pop, ain't-it Rosey? but it's Sleight, sure enough, all the time. This yer check," he added, producing a paper from the depths of the wallet, "this yer check for 25,000 dollars is wot he paid for it only two hours ago."

"But," said Renshaw, springing to his feet furiously, "you're duped, swindled — betrayed!"

"Young man," said Nott, throwing a certain dignity into his habitual gesture of placing his hands on Renshaw's shoulders, "I bought this yer ship five years ago jist ez she stood for 8,000 dollars. Kalkilatin' wot she cost me in repairs and taxes, and wot she brought me in since then, accordin' to my figgerin', I don't call a clear profit of 15,000 dollars much of a swindle."

"Tell him all," said Rosey, quickly, more alarmed at Renshaw's despairing face than at the news itself. "Tell him everything, Dick — Mr. Renshaw; it may not be too late."

In a voice half choked with passionate indignation Renshaw hurriedly repeated the story of the hidden treasure, and the plot to rescue it, prompted frequently by Rosey's tenacious memory and assisted by Rosey's deft and tactful explanations. But to their surprise the imperturbable countenance of Abner Nott never altered; a slight moisture of kindly paternal tolerance of their extravagance glistened in his little eyes, but nothing more.

" Ef there was a part o' this ship, a plank or a bolt ez I don't know, ez I hev n't touched with my own hand, and looked into with my own eyes, thar might be suthin' in that story. I don't let on to be a sailor like *you*, but ez I know the ship ez a boy knows his first hoss, as a woman knows her first babby, I reckon thar ain't no treasure yer, onless it was brought into the Pontiac last night by them chaps."

" But are you mad ! Sleight would not pay three times the value of the ship to-day if he were not positive ! And that positive knowledge was gained last night by the villain who broke into the Pontiac — no doubt the Lascar."

" Surely," said Nott, meditatively. " The Lascar ! There 's suthin' in that. That Lascar I fastened down in the hold last night unbeknownst to you, Mr. Renshaw, and let him out again this morning ekally unbeknownst."

"And you let him carry his information to Sleight — without a word!" said Renshaw, with a sickening sense of Nott's utter fatuity.

"I sent him back with a message to the man he kem from," said Nott, winking both his eyes at Renshaw, significantly, and making signs behind his daughter's back.

Rosey, conscious of her lover's irritation, and more eager to soothe his impatience than from any faith in her suggestion, interfered. "Why not examine the place where he was concealed? he may have left some traces of his search."

The two men looked at each other. "Seein' ez I've turned the Pontiac over to Sleight jist ez it stands, I don't know ez it's 'zactly on the square," said Nott doubtfully.

"You've a right to know at least *what* you deliver to him," interrupted Renshaw brusquely: "Bring a lantern."

Followed by Rosey, Renshaw and Nott hurriedly sought the lower deck and the

open hatch of the forehold. The two men
leaped down first with the lantern, and then
assisted Rosey to descend. Renshaw took a
step forward and uttered a cry.

The rays of the lantern fell on the ship's
side. The Lascar had, during his forced
seclusion, put back the boxes of treasure
and replaced the planking, yet not so carefully but that the quick eye of Renshaw had
discovered it. The next moment he had
stripped away the planking again, and the
hurriedly-restored box which the Lascar had
found fell to the deck, scattering part of its
ringing contents. Rosey turned pale; Renshaw's eyes flashed fire; only Abner Nott
remained quiet and impassive.

" Are you satisfied you have been duped?"
said Renshaw passionately.

To their surprise Mr. Nott stooped down,
and picking up one of the coins handed it
gravely to Renshaw. " Would ye mind
heftin' that 'ere coin in your hand — feelin'
it, bitin' it, scrapin' it with a knife, and

17

kinder seein' how it compares with other coins?"

"What do you mean?" said Renshaw.

"I mean that that yer coin — that *all* the coins in this yer box, that all the coins in them other boxes — and ther's forty on 'em — is all and every one of 'em counterfeits!"

The piece dropped unconsciously from Renshaw's hand, and striking another that lay on the deck gave out a dull, suspicious ring.

"They waz counterfeits got up by them Dutch supercargo sharps for dealin' with the Injins and cannibals and South Sea heathens ez bows down to wood and stone. It satisfied them ez well ez them buttons ye puts in missionary boxes, I reckon, and 'cepting ez freight, don't cost nothin'. I found 'em tucked in the ribs o' the old Pontiac when I bought her, and I nailed 'em up in thar lest they should fall into dishonest hands. It's a lucky thing, Mr. Renshaw, that they comes into the honest fingers of a square man like Sleight — ain't it?"

He turned his small, guileless eyes upon
Renshaw with such child-like simplicity that
it checked the hysterical laugh that was rising to the young man's lips.

" But did any one know of this but yourself ? "

" I reckon not. I once suspicioned that
old Cap'en Bowers, who was always foolin'
round the hold yer, must hev noticed the
bulge in the casin', but when he took to
axin' questions I axed others — ye know my
style, Rosey ?   Come."

He led the way grimly back to the cabin,
the young people following ; but turning
suddenly at the companion way he observed
Renshaw's arm around the waist of his
daughter. He said nothing until they had
reached the cabin, when he closed the door
softly, and looking at them both gently, said
with infinite cunning —

" Ef it is n't too late, Rosey, ye kin tell
this young man ez how I forgive him for
havin' diskivered THE TREASURE of the
Pontiac."

.   .   .   .

It was nearly eighteen months afterwards that Mr. Nott one morning entered the room of his son-in-law at Mandroño Cottage. Drawing him aside, he said with his old air of mystery, " Now ez Rosey's ailin' and don't seem to be so eager to diskiver what's become of Mr. Ferrers, I don't mind tellin' ye that over a year ago I heard he died suddenly in Sacramento. Thar was suthin' in the paper about his bein' a lunatic and claimin' to be a relation to somebody on the Pontiac; but likes ez not it's only the way those newspaper fellows got hold of the story of his wantin' to marry Rosey."